'No,' she whispered. 'I don't want to wake up beside you.'

Something shuttered in his face—an expression she didn't like. Pain? No. It was a closing of something that had barely started to open.

'Jake, no,' she said swiftly—she did *not* want to hurt this man, but this was important. She was struggling to explain it, struggling to understand it herself, but somehow she had to find words for what she was feeling. 'What happened tonight was magic, time out of frame. I needed it so much—I needed you—and I'll be grateful for the rest of my life. But if I wake up beside you in the morning... then I might hold and cling. I don't want that. I don't want anything to mess with what we had tonight.'

I don't want to fall in love.

Where had that come from? No matter, it was there, hovering between them as if both had thought it.

Love... After one night? She didn't think so.

She knew she had to move on. Somehow Jake seemed to have given her the strength to do just that, and she would not mess with it.

'I loved tonight,' she whispered. 'Tonight I loved you. But we both know our worlds don't fit together. Let's just accept tonight's magic and move on.'

'I'm not sure I can.' He was pushing open the door to her bedroom with his foot...

Dear Reader

On February 7th 2009, wildfire destroyed a vast section of Australia's south-east corner. Almost two hundred lives were lost, many people lost their homes, and vast tracts of farmland and natural bushland were destroyed. But in the days that followed we saw our community at its best.

I was privileged to be part of a livestock appeal, and the response left us overwhelmed by human kindness. People brought in birdseed and cuttlefish, and others staggered in under huge bags of dog food. We had people who looked as if they had no money at all coming in with animal bedding, food—anything they could think of. We had companies donating truckloads of their produce. We had vets arriving with veterinary equipment.

Volunteers loaded, unloaded, distributed. Out in the burned-out bushland volunteers scattered feed, searched for injured animals, did whatever was needed. Volunteers are working still.

In Tori's story I wanted to share with you some of my pride in my community, and my awe of what people are capable of. From the ashes springs new life. Take care of each other, but know that in times of deepest trouble we're never truly alone.

And we can still look forward to love.

Marion Lennox

DATING THE MILLIONAIRE DOCTOR

BY
MARION LENNOX

™MILLS & BOON®

First published in Great Britain 2010
Harlequin Mills & Boon Limited,
Eton House, 18-24 Paradise Road, Richmond, Surrey TW9 1SR

© Marion Lennox 2010

ISBN: 978 0 263 21511 3

Marion Lennox is a country girl, born on an Australian dairy farm. She moved on—mostly because the cows just weren't interested in her stories! Married to a 'very special doctor', Marion writes romances for Mills & Boon® Medical™ Romance as well as Mills & Boon® pt Romance (she used a different name for each category for a while—if you're looking for her past Mills & Boon® Romance stories, search for author Trisha David as well).

In her non-writing life Marion cares for kids, cats, dogs, chooks and goldfish. She travels, she fights her rampant garden (she's losing) and her house dust (she's lost).

Having spun in circles for the first part of her life, she's now stepped back from her 'other' career, which was teaching statistics at her local university. Finally she's reprioritised her life, figured out what's important and discovered the joys of deep baths, romance and chocolate. Preferably all at the same time!

Recent titles by the same author:

Mills & Boon® Medical™ Romance

CITY SURGEON, SMALL TOWN MIRACLE
A SPECIAL KIND OF FAMILY

Mills & Boon® Romance

CINDERELLA: HIRED BY THE PRINCE
CROWNED: THE PALACE NANNY
  (*Marrying His Majesty* mini-series)

This book is dedicated to all the wonderful volunteers
who worked tirelessly to save injured wildlife
after the Australian Black Saturday bushfires.

CHAPTER ONE

FIVE-MINUTE dating was five minutes too long. He'd dated nine women tonight, and the last was the least inspiring of the lot.

Jake glanced down at his fact sheet, hoping for help. *Victoria. Twenty-nine. Single.* There wasn't a lot here to talk about.

'I'm pleased to meet you, Victoria,' he ventured. That's terrific, he thought wryly. Snappy dialogue. Incisive. Excellent way to start things rolling.

'My friends call me Tori,' she ventured, dragging her gaze from the door. Was she thinking about escaping?

'Is this your first try at speed dating?'

'Yes. And you?'

'Yes.'

This wasn't exactly scintillating, he conceded. Where did he go from here?

Each of his last nine 'dates' had been vivacious and chirpy. He hadn't needed to make an effort. Now, when effort was required, he wondered whether it was worth it.

Had Tori made an effort?

Victoria—or Tori—looked a real country mouse. She was wearing a knee-length black skirt, scuffed court shoes and a white blouse with ruffles down the front. Her chestnut-brown curls—had she cut the fringe herself?—had been pulled into a rough knot, simply tied with a white ribbon. She wore no make up and no jewellery.

Why was she here if she wasn't prepared to spend some time on her appearance? he wondered. The lines around her clear green eyes were stretched tight, making her seem a lot older than twenty-nine years. But did she care? She looked as if she wanted to be here even less than he did, which was really saying something.

The manager of Dr. Jake Hunter's Australian properties had promised Jake he'd enjoy it, but enjoy was so far off the mark Jake couldn't believe it. But he was here. He was stuck. He had to make conversation.

'So what do you do for a living?'

'I care for injured wildlife.'

That'd be right. She looked like a do-gooder. Not that he had anything against do-gooders, he reminded himself hastily. It was just that she looked…the type.

'So you'll have been busy in the fires?'

'Yes.'

And here was another conversation stopper. Six months ago wildfire had ripped this little community apart, decimating the entire district. As an outsider Jake didn't know where to take it. Should he say something like, Was your house burned? Was anyone you cared about hurt?

Surely the fact that she'd come to speed dating was proof that it hadn't touched her too badly. But don't go there, he told himself, and he didn't. Which left silence.

'What…what about you?' she asked, sounding desperate, and he thought, Three minutes and fifty seconds left.

'I live in the U.S. but I own properties here, in the valley and up on the ridge. I've come back now to check on them, maybe put them on the market.'

'Were they damaged?'

'Not badly. My manager's been taking care of them for me. He's the one who talked me into coming tonight.'

'So speed dating's not your thing?'

'No,' he admitted, and decided to be honest. She looked the sort of woman who called a spade a spade. 'Rob said you were a guy short. I got dragged into this at the last minute.'

'You don't want to be here?'

'No.'

'Then I'm wasting your time,' she said, and suddenly the mouse had changed into something else entirely. Her relief was palpable. She rose and took his hand in a grip so firm it surprised him. 'This is the last round so we can finish this now. Goodnight, Jake.'

Then, astonishingly, she smiled, a wide, white smile that had the power to turn her face from plain to something extraordinary. But he didn't have a chance to register the smile for long. She'd released his hand and was heading for the door, her sensible heels clicking briskly on the polished wooden floorboards of the Combadeen Hall.

And to his further bewilderment, the moment she rose she looked...cute? Definitely cute, he thought. Her curls bounced on her shoulders. She had curves in all the right places, the badly fitting skirt unable to conceal her tiny waist, the lovely lines of her legs and the unconscious wiggle of her hips as she stalked to the door.

He wasn't the only one watching. As she tugged the door open and walked out into the night, as the door slammed closed behind her, he realised everyone else in the hall was looking as well, as astonished as he was.

He'd just been stood up for a speed date. He'd been stood up by a smile that was truly stunning.

Should he follow?

Um, no. She was right. Speed dating was not his thing.

Nor was any other sort of dating, he acknowledged. He

was in town to check on his father's property, to sign documents to put the farmhouse on the ridge on the market and to make a decision about the resort. Then he was out of here. His job back in the States was waiting. He had no place here.

So why was he watching a country mouse stalk away from him, as if he cared?

Why had she come?

Her best friend, Barb, had lied to her. They can't have been a woman short if that guy—Jake?—could patronise her by saying he was only here to make up numbers, to do them all a favour.

Arrogant toerag.

Outside, the stars were hanging low in the sky. The air was crisp and clean, and she filled her lungs, as if the hall inside had been full of smoke.

Of course it wasn't, though maybe the smell of smoke would never completely leave her. The fire that had ripped through these mountains had changed her life—and she wasn't ready to move on, no matter what Barb said.

'Please come tonight,' Barb had pleaded. 'We're desperate to make up the numbers. It'll be fun. Come on, Tori, life can be good again. You can try.'

So she'd tried. Not very hard, she conceded, looking ruefully down at her serviceable skirt. She'd been living courtesy of welfare bins for too long now.

Tori—or more formally Dr. Victoria Nicholls, veterinary surgeon—had no financial need of welfare bins, but the outpouring of the Australian public had been massive. The local hall was filled with clothes donated to replace what was burned, and it was easier to grab what she needed than to waste time shopping.

She hadn't shopped since…

She shook herself. Don't go there.

But maybe she had to go there. Maybe that was part of the healing. No, she hadn't shopped since the fire. She hadn't dated since the fire—or before, of course, but then she'd had Toby. Or she'd thought she'd had Toby. There was the king of all toerags. Even the thought of him made her cringe. That she could have imagined herself in love with him...

She'd been incredibly, appallingly dumb. She'd made one disastrous mistake that had cost her everything, so what on earth was she doing lining up for another?

Oh, for heaven's sake, she was supposed to be moving on. There were good people out there, she told herself. Good men. She had to learn to trust again. Jake had seemed...

Bored. Compelled to be there. But sort of interesting?

Maybe Barb was right; she did need to get out more, because Jake seemed to have stirred something in her that hadn't been stirred for a long time.

He'd been long and lean and sort of...sculpted. Rangy. He hadn't bothered to shave, and there was another mark against him. She'd gone to all the trouble of finding this stupid blouse and he'd come with a five-o'clock shadow. Mind, it had looked incredibly sexy, with his deep, black hair—a little bit wavy—and his lovely brown eyes and the crinkles around his tanned face that said he normally didn't look as bored as this; normally he smiled.

How stupid was this? She gave herself an angry shake. She'd met ten men tonight, all of them seemed uninterested and uninteresting, and even though Jake seemed...interesting...he was the rudest of the lot.

She'd been stupid once. Any relationship she might have in the future must thus be dictated by sense and not by hormones, and all she'd felt with Jake was hormones. Lots of hormones.

Disgusted, she climbed into her battered van and headed out of the car park, back up the mountain. She'd been away for long enough.

No matter what Barb said, she wasn't ready for a new life. She already had an all-consuming one.

Or did she? Barb was right, she accepted. The life she knew was coming to an end.

Where did she go from here?

Wherever—as long as her decisions were based on sense and not hormones, she told herself fiercely and headed back up the mountain.

'Anyone strike your fancy?'

Jake's manager and friend from university days was watching a blonde totter across the car park to her cute little sports car. She was definitely Rob's choice for the night. Maybe he'd even take it further.

As opposed to Jake. He had no intention of ever taking things further. Yeah, it had been crazy to agree to speed dating. He was here for less than a week, and every one of the women he'd met tonight had diamonds in their eyes.

He didn't do diamonds. Diamonds had been drilled out of him early.

Jake had been brought up by a mother who spent her life bewailing an Australian father who was, according to her, the lowest form of life on the planet. Love made you cry, his mother told him, over and over from the time he was a toddler, since she'd taken him back to the States and—as she'd said repeatedly—abandoned her dreams for ever.

Maybe his mother's broken dreams had left their legacy. Who knew? He needed a shrink to tell him, but a shrink couldn't change him. He didn't do long-term relationships. He'd never felt the slightest need to take things down that road. Women were colleagues and friends. They were often great companions. The occasional mutually casual relationship was great, but why open yourself to the angst of commitment?

Rob, however, had talked about tonight as though it was the answer to his prayers. As if diamonds were on his agenda. Which was ridiculous.

'What do you see in this five-minute set-up?' he demanded, and Rob gave a crooked smile.

'My perfect woman's out there somewhere. I just have to find her. So there was no one tonight who struck your fancy?'

'Your lady's hot,' Jake conceded, being generous. 'But no.'

'So what did you say to Doc Nicholls?' Rob asked. 'To make her walk out.'

'Doc Nicholls?'

'Tori. Barb says she's the vet up on the ridge, part of the group that rent your house. I'm thinking I should have met her before this, but since the fires life's been crazy. Any negotiation's been done through Barb. Then tonight…I couldn't make her talk, but at least she stayed the full five minutes. Unlike you. You didn't say anything to upset her, did you? Barb'll have me hung, drawn and quartered if you've hurt her feelings.'

'How could I have hurt her feelings?'

'You say it like it is,' Rob said. 'Not always best.'

'I don't tell lies, if that's what you mean.'

'So what did you tell her?'

'Just that I was here to make up the numbers.'

'Right,' Rob said. 'That'd be a turn-on. I'm speed dating because I'm being kind. Woo-hoo.'

'Look, it doesn't matter anyway,' Jake said, shoving his hands into his pockets and staring out at the vast night sky. Hankering for Manhattan where stars were in shop windows and not straight up. 'I'll get the house on the market and leave again, though I don't know why you can't do it for me.'

'I offered, if you remember, and for once you decided to take an interest and come do it yourself.'

'The figure seemed ludicrously low.'

'Who wants a house on top of a fire-prone ridge?'

'It was snapped up pretty fast after the fires.'

'Only because there was still green feed around it,' Rob said bluntly. 'And you offered it rent free. But six months on, there's feed everywhere, and it's smoke damaged. Property values on the ridge will rise again but not until the memory of the fire fades a bit. So many of the people round here lost someone. You're lucky you weren't living here yourself.'

Yeah, well… Luck had all sorts of guises, Jake thought, as they headed back down the valley towards the second property his father had left him—a lodge with attached vineyard. His mother would definitely say he was lucky not to live here. His mother would be devastated that he was here now.

But how could he help but come? Jake was wealthy before his father died, but his father's death had made him more so. The combined properties, even at post-fire prices, were worth a fortune.

Why had he held onto them? That was a question he was having trouble facing, and maybe that's why he was here— seeking some final connection to his father.

Apart from financial support—given grudgingly, according to his mother—Jake's father had played no part in his life. He hadn't contacted him all through his childhood. There'd been nothing. But twelve years ago, when Jake qualified as a doctor, he'd finally received a letter. Congratulating him and wishing him all the best for his future. Intrigued, he'd written back. That's when he'd discovered his father was working as a country doctor in the hills outside Melbourne.

He'd decided he wouldn't mind getting a personal idea about this man who'd cared for him financially but in no other sense. Tentatively he'd suggested a visit.

But, 'I hear your mother's ill and she'd hate it,' his father had said bluntly. 'I've married again. We've all moved on.

After all these years, what's the point? I'm glad you've gradu-
ated and I'm proud of you. I'm sorry I haven't been able to
contact you before, but now I have…let's leave it there.'

So he'd left it, and then life grew busy. He'd immersed
himself in his career. He'd visit Australia one day, he
promised himself, but then five years ago his father died,
suddenly, of a massive coronary.

Jake had finally come then, to a funeral that shocked him
with the community outpouring of grief. He'd sat at the back
of the church and watched strangers cry for a father he didn't
know. A father who hadn't even objected when his mother
had changed his name back to hers. Who seemed to have little
connection to him at all.

But when tentatively he'd confessed to the elderly lady beside
him who he was, to his astonishment she'd known all about him.

'I'm one of Old Doc's patients—and you must be Jake,'
she'd said, sniffing and beaming a watery smile at him. 'His
American son. Doc had a baby picture of you up on his clinic
wall. I used to say to him it was a shame your mother took
you away, but he'd say, "Just because he's in the States doesn't
make him any less my son. I love him wherever he is."'

He'd loved him? That was the first he'd heard of it. The
woman had wanted to introduce him around, but he was so
shocked he'd simply walked away.

Maybe he should have sold the properties then, but it had
seemed wrong. Troubled by the conflicting messages he was
getting—had his father indeed cared?—and by the morality
of accepting such an inheritance, he'd employed Rob to
manage the properties and he'd retreated to the States. To his
all-consuming career as chief anaesthetist at Manhattan
Central.

But now, finally, he'd returned.

The lodge, once owned by his stepmother and run as a
winery and genteel place of retreat, had been needed as emer-

gency accommodation in the first weeks after the fire. Rob had it running again now, but there were few guests.

Rob had worked in hospitality for years. Five years back he'd followed a lady to Australia—of course—and jumped at the opportunity to run the lodge, but getting it viable again could take more than Rob's enthusiasm. And up on the ridge, Jake's second property—the one used by Tori and her friends—was smoke damaged and had been used for six months as an animal hospital.

So maybe he should sell both. Maybe he should abandon any last trace of a father he didn't know, abandon any last connection. Rob would find alternative employment. His friend was born hopeful. The blonde's car was in front of them, and Rob was speeding up and slowing down, doing a bit of automotive courting. Jake shook his head in disbelief.

'Hey, stop it with the disapproval.' Rob grinned, sensing his thoughts. 'Worry about your own love life.'

'I don't have a love life.'

'Exactly. My life's work, wine and women. Your life's medicine, medicine and medicine—and worry. You know you don't need to. The resort will turn around.'

'Maybe it will,' Jake agreed and then thought, Why *was* he worrying? The winery supported the lodge, he had no money problems, so why was he even here? And the farmhouse up on the ridge—Old Doc's Place, the locals called it— well, why was he quibbling about price? 'I'll go check out the ridge tomorrow, put it on the market and then go home.'

'Back to your medicine.'

'It's what I do.'

'It's what you are,' Rob said. 'Why do you think I conned you into coming tonight? You need a life.'

'I have a life.'

'Right,' Rob drawled in a voice that said he didn't believe it at all. 'Sure thing.'

CHAPTER TWO

SHE was losing the fight—and someone was banging on the front door. Her nurse's gaze shifted towards the entrance, her brows raised in enquiry.

'Leave it,' Tori said tightly. 'She's slipping.'

Up until now the koala under her hands had been responding well. Like so many animals, she'd been caught up in the wildfire, but she was one of the lucky ones, found by firefighters the day after the fire, brought into Tori's care and gradually rehabilitated.

Tori had worked hard with her, and up until now she'd thought she'd survive. But then a few days ago she'd found a tiny abscess in the scar tissue on her leg. Despite antibiotics and the best of care, it was spreading. It needed careful debridement under anaesthetic. That left a problem. With this shelter winding down, she no longer had full veterinary support.

If she took her down the mountain she could get another veterinarian to assist, but travel often took more of a toll on injured animals than the procedure itself. Thus she was working with Becky, a competent veterinary nurse who worked under instruction. It wasn't enough. She needed an expert, right here, right now, who could respond to minute-by-minute changes in the koala's condition.

She was working as fast as she could to get the edges of the abscess clean but she couldn't work fast enough. The little animal was slipping. To lose her after all this time… She was starting to feel sick.

'Anyone there?' It was a deep masculine voice, calling from the hallway. Whoever had knocked had come right in.

The door to their improvised operating theatre opened. Tori glanced up, ready to yell at whoever it was to get out—and it was Jake. Her one-and-a-half-minute date.

Whatever. It could be the king himself and there was only one reaction. 'Out,' she snapped, and Becky said, 'I think she's stopped breathing.'

Her attention switched back to her koala. She could have wept. To lose her now…

'Can I help?' Jake demanded.

She shook her head, hardly conscious that she was responding. She had to intubate. But if she left the wound… She couldn't do both jobs herself.

'Unless you can intubate…' she whispered, hopeless. She shouldn't have tried. The oral conformation of koalas—small mouth, narrow dental arcade, a long, soft palate and a caudally placed glottal opening, all of these combined with a propensity to low blood oxygen saturation—made koala anaesthetics risky at the best of times. And without another vet…

'I can intubate,' he snapped. 'Keep working.'

'You can?'

Jake was already at the side bench, staring down at equipment. 'What size tube?'

'Four millimetre,' she said automatically.

Another vet? Maybe he was, she thought, as he grabbed equipment and headed to the table. Whoever he was, he knew what he was doing.

The soft palate of the koalas obscures the epiglottis from

direct view, but Jake didn't hesitate. He'd found and was using silicone spray, snapping instructions at Becky to hand him equipment.

Tori was concentrating on applying pressure to the wound to prevent more blood loss. She was therefore able to watch in awed amazement as Jake manoeuvered the little animal into a sternal recumbency position, as he applied more spray—and as he slid the tube home.

It was like the Angel Gabriel had suddenly appeared from the heavens. Ask and ye shall receive. She'd barely been aware that she'd prayed.

No matter where he'd come from, no matter that she couldn't see his wings and he sounded autocratic and fierce rather than soft and halo-like, her one-and-a-half-minute date was definitely assuming angel-like status. He had oxygen flowing in what seemed seconds. The monitor by Tori's side showed a slight shift in the thin blue line—and then a major one.

She had life.

'Heart rate's seventy beats a minute,' Jake snapped, adjusting the flow. 'How does that compare to normal?'

Not a vet, then? Or not a vet who cared for koalas. Of course not.

'Low, but a whole lot better than before you arrived,' she told him, but there was no time for questions. Stunned, she went back to what she was doing. She was incredibly grateful but now wasn't the time to show it. She had to get this wound debrided, then get it dressed so the anaesthetic could be reversed.

Koalas died under anaesthetic. This one wouldn't. Please…

As if in echo of her thoughts, Jake said, 'She seems knocked around. Wouldn't euthanasia be the kindest option?' He'd had time now to take in the scar tissue, the signs of major trauma.

'Says the man who just saved her,' Tori muttered. 'Let's try to keep her alive until I finish. We can do the moral debate later.'

'Right.'

There was silence while she worked on. Becky had faded into the background, assisting both of them, deeply relieved, Tori guessed, to be freed from a task she hated. There was so much they'd done in the past six months they'd all hated—including putting down more animals than she wanted to think about.

How to explain that after so much death, one life became disproportionately important. This little one she was working on didn't have a name. Or…she shouldn't give her one. She should not be emotionally involved.

Only, of course, she *was* emotionally involved. Koala Number Thirty-seven—the thirty-seventh koala she'd treated since the fire—belonged in the wild, and Tori was determined to get her back there. She would win this last battle. She must.

Thanks to this man, she just might.

Who was he?

She was finishing now, applying dressings, having enough time again to pay attention to the man at the head of the table. He was watching the monitors like a hawk, his face fierce, absorbed, totally committed to what he was doing.

Inserting an endotracheal tube in a koala was always dangerous territory. If you went too deep there was a major risk of traumatising the trachea and extending the tube into bronchus. She hadn't told him that. There hadn't been time, but he'd seemed to know it instinctively. How?

Maybe he was a vet, or maybe he did paediatric anaesthesia. Sometimes she thought paediatrics and veterinary science were inexplicably linked. Varying weights and sizes. The inability of the patient to explain where the pain was.

Who was he?

She was finished. Another check of the monitors. Pulse rate eighty. Blood oxygen saturation ninety percent.

Koala Thirty-seven just might live.

She couldn't help herself; she put her hand on the soft fur of the little koala's face and bestowed a silent blessing.

'You keep on living,' she whispered. 'You've come so far. You will make it.'

'She might well,' Jake said. He was working surely and confidently, removing the endotracheal tube with care and watching with satisfaction as the little animal settled back into normal breathing pattern. 'So who's going to pay her bill?'

'Now there's a question,' she murmured. She was carrying the little animal carefully back to her cage in the corner. She wasn't out of the woods yet—she knew that. Any procedure took it out of these wild animals, but at least there was hope.

She'd done all she could, she thought, arranging the IV line the little animal needed to provide fluids until she started eating again. Then she was finished.

Really finished, she thought suddenly. There was now nothing left to do.

The sensation was strange. For the six months since the fires Tori had worked nonstop. This place had been a refuge for injured wildlife from all over the mountain. They'd had up to fifty volunteers at one time, with Tori supervising the care of as many as three hundred animals. Kangaroos, wallabies, possums, cockatoos, koalas—so many koalas. So many battles. So much loss.

It was over. Those who could be saved had been saved, and were being re-introduced in the wild. The spring rains had come, the bush was regenerating; there was food and water out there for animals to re-establish territories.

This little koala was the last of her responsibilities. She glanced down at her and, as she did, she felt a wave of the deep grief that was always with her. All those she'd failed…

'Is it okay if I go now?' Becky said, glancing uncertainly at Jake. 'It's just…Ben's picking me up. He'll be waiting.'

'Sure, Becky. Thanks for your help.'

'You won't need me again, will you?'

'No.' She glanced back at the koala. If there was a need for more surgery, she knew what her decision would have to be, and for that she wouldn't need Becky.

'See you, then,' Becky said. 'I'm out of here. Hooray for the city—I'm so over this place.' And with another curious glance at Jake she disappeared, closing the door behind her.

Leaving Tori with Jake.

'I… Thank you,' she managed. He looked pretty much like he had the night before. Slightly more casual. Faded jeans and a white, open-necked shirt. Elastic-sided boots. He looked like a local, she thought, which was at odds with his American accent.

'My pleasure,' he said, and sounded like he meant it. 'I didn't realise last night that you were a vet.'

'I didn't know you were.'

'I'm not.'

'So inserting endotracheal tubes in koalas is just a splinter skill for, say, a television repairman?'

'I'm an anaesthetist. Jake Hunter.'

'An anaesthetist,' Tori said blankly. 'In Combadeen? You have to be kidding.'

'I'm not kidding. I'm staying at Manwillinbah Lodge.'

'Rob Winston's place?' She was struggling now with the connection. What had Jake said last night? 'I own properties here, in the valley and up on the ridge.' And Rob. Distracted, she thought of the pleasant young man who'd flirted outrageously last night. She remembered him arriving with this man. With Jake. 'Was Rob Winston the ninth date last night?' she demanded.

'That was Rob.'

'He was nice. Fun.'

'Meaning, I wasn't?'

'I didn't say that. But I wish I'd known who he was,' she said ruefully. 'He should have told me. I need to thank him, and not only for letting us use this place. I had a friend who went to Manwillinbah Lodge when she was released from hospital two months ago. It wasn't right for her. She needed ongoing medical treatment, but that wasn't Rob's fault, and she said he tried so hard to give her time out. So many people around here need that.' She frowned, figuring more things out. 'So is this…is this your farm?'

'It is.'

'Oh, my…'

Uh-oh.

Last night she'd walked out on her landlord. On the guy who'd made this whole hospital possible. 'You've been giving this place to us rent free and I didn't even know who you were.' It was practically a wail and he grinned.

'This is a whole new conversation topic. If we'd known last night we could have used our whole five minutes.'

She managed a smile—just. How embarrassing. And how to retrieve the situation?

She should shake his hand. Or, um, not. She glanced down at her gloves and decided gratitude needed to wait. Plus she needed to catch her breath. Breath seemed in remarkably short supply.

'Could you excuse me for a moment?' she muttered. 'I need to wash.' And she disappeared—she almost ran— leaving him alone with Koala Number Thirty-seven.

He was in the front room of what seemed to have been a grand old farmhouse. It still was, somewhere under the litter of what looked to be an animal hospital.

When the fires had ripped through here, almost fifty

percent of properties on the ridge had been destroyed. The loss of life and property had been so massive there'd been international television coverage. Horrified, he'd contacted Rob to see how he could help.

'The lodge and the winery are okay,' Rob told him. 'We're almost ten miles from where the fire front turned back on itself, so apart from smoke on the grapes there's little damage. I've been asked if we can provide emergency accommodation, if it's okay with you. And the farmhouse on the ridge… There's an animal-welfare place wanting headquarters. When the wind shifted, pushing the fire back on itself, your place was spared. Just. There's still feed around it, and the house itself is basically okay, but your tenants are moving off the mountain. They can't cope with the mess and the smell, and they're going to her mother's. Can the animal-welfare people use it for six months or so?'

'Of course,' he'd said, so it was now a hospital—of sorts.

But as he looked around he thought he wouldn't have minded seeing it as it once was—a gracious family home. And he wouldn't have minded seeing the bushland around here as it was either. The fire had burned to within fifty yards of the house and then turned. Beyond that demarcation, the bush was black and skeletal. Green tinges were showing through the ash now, alleviating the blackness, but six months ago it must have been a nightmare.

He stared out the window until Tori bustled back into the room, carrying a bucket of steaming, soapy water. She looked like a woman who didn't stay still for long, he thought. Busy. Clinically efficient. Cute?

Definitely still cute. She was in ancient jeans, an even more ancient T-shirt and a white clinical coat with a torn pocket. Her curls were again scraped back into a ponytail. Last night she'd pulled them back with a ribbon. Today they were tied with an elastic band. She looked…workmanlike.

But workmanlike or not, he thought, nothing could hide her inherent sexiness. Why had he wasted time last night thinking she was dowdy?

When she left the room she'd looked confused. Now, however, she looked relieved, as if she'd spent her bucket-filling time figuring things out as well.

'I know now why you're here,' she told him. 'You're Old Doc's son. Jake. I loved your father.' She hesitated as if she wanted to say something else, but then thought better of it.

'So you're here to put this farm on the market,' she continued briskly. 'That's fine, but first I need to thank you.' She abandoned her bucket, put her hands out and grasped his, holding them in the same strong grip of the night before, a grip that made him wonder how he'd ever thought her a mouse. The connection felt strangely…right.

But Tori wasn't noticing connections. She was moving right on.

'I can't tell you how grateful we've been,' she said. 'It's been fabulous—and Barb said you won't take any rent. It's been truly lifesaving.' She looked across at the little koala in her cage, and her business-like tone faltered a little. 'And now you'll sell. That's fine. We don't need it any more. As soon as this one goes…'

'She's the only one here now?'

'We release as soon as we can,' she said, efficient again. 'Wild animals respond to captivity with stress. There's a few that are too damaged to survive on their own, but we've re-located them all now to bigger animal shelters. Places where they can have as close to a normal life as possible. So yes, there's only this little one here now. And me.'

He frowned. 'You're living here?'

'I… Yes. I hope you don't mind. It's easier.'

'You're on twenty–four-hour call?'

'Not many of my patients buzz me. It's not as hard as it

sounds.' She was opening the door onto the verandah and ushering him out, almost before he was aware of what she was doing.

There was a small dog lying on an ancient settee by the door. He'd seen him as he arrived. He was some sort of terrier, a nondescript brown-and-white mutt who hadn't bothered checking Jake out when he arrived. Too old to care? He glanced up now, gave a feeble wag of his tail and then went back to what he was doing.

Which wasn't sleeping, Jake realised. He was staring down the valley, as if he was waiting for someone.

Tori touched the dog's ears, and the dog nosed her palm and went right back to looking. Waiting to go home?

'You'll be looking forwards to going home,' he ventured, and saw flash of pain, hidden fast. Uh-oh, he thought. Stupid. If she was staying here... She'd be one of the hundreds burned out.

She hesitated and he knew he was right, but it was too late to retrieve the situation. 'I guess I must be,' she said slowly before he could think what else to say, and she shrugged. 'No, of course I am. It's time I moved on.'

'Is that what you were doing last night—moving on?'

'What I was doing last night was being conned by my friend. I gather you were conned as well. So when do you need me to move out?'

'I don't—'

'It'll be soon. You'll need to clean the place up before you put it on the market. There's a lot of smoke damage. Do you want to look through now?' She glanced at her watch. 'I have a teleconference in five minutes with our local shelter staffers, but you could look around yourself.'

'I'd be happier if you could show me personally.'

Why had he said that? Surely he could see what he needed from here. What point was there doing a detailed inspection, and why did he need a personal tour from Tori?

She had him fascinated. There was something about the way her hand had shaken his, brisk, efficient, but also…there was something vulnerable about her. Something he couldn't figure out.

She wasn't sounding vulnerable, though. She was organising. 'I can show you,' she said, 'but if you want the personal tour it'll have to be later in the day. But tomorrow would be better.'

'Is nine in the morning all right?'

'Sure. When are you going back to the States?'

'Monday.' Six days away.

Suddenly six days seemed okay. If he kept the resort there was only this place to organise. He could be here again tomorrow and be shown over the property by Tori. Those jeans… He'd never seen jeans look this good on a woman.

'I do need to get in to my teleconference,' she said, a bit sharply, and he pulled himself together. What was he thinking? This woman was a country mouse—a vet who lived on the other side of the world to him. If she hadn't stood him up on a five-minute date…

Was that what this was? Bruised ego?

'Thank you very much for saving my koala,' she said, starting to edge away.

'What's she called?'

'I don't name them. You get attached if you name them.'

'You don't get attached?'

'I try hard not to. Now if you'll excuse me…'

'Of course,' he said, but he was still surprised when she stepped back inside the house and closed the door sharply behind her.

She wasn't a time waster, then, Dr. Nicholls. He didn't waste time either—but he couldn't help feeling piqued. Most women reacted to him differently to the way this woman had.

What was he thinking?

Nothing. There was nothing to think about. He gave himself a mental swipe to the side of the head and headed back to his rental car. He should get back to the States fast if he thought shabby little country vets were cute. If he thought shabby little country vets were fascinating.

He wasn't to know that one shabby little country vet watched him until he was out of sight.

Boy, was she hopeless. She twitched the smoke-stained drapes back into place and glowered at nothing in particular. One gorgeous male, and here she was, feeling…weird. Which was dumb. The last thing she needed in her life was another man.

So why had she let Barb talk her into five-minute dating?

Because, with the leaving of the army of volunteers, she'd become so lonely she was starting to talk to walls.

Dad. Micki.

Don't go there.

There weren't even enough animals left to talk to. She returned to the makeshift surgery and stooped to check the little koala. She was barely conscious. So small. So battered.

Maybe it had been a mistake to keep on trying.

'Live,' she whispered, almost fiercely. 'You must get better. You must start living again.'

She knew she must, too.

She glanced out the window to the west and flinched like she always did. She could just see the chimney stack which was all that was left of the house she'd lived in forever.

Her dad. Her sister.

'Move on,' she whispered. 'Get yourself a nice little town house in the city. You can be a pet vet. Take care of allergies, dew claws, vaccinations.'

Maybe she would. It was just…she didn't feel ready yet.

In a couple of weeks this little koala should be ready to move on to a wildlife refuge and this place would be sold to be a home again. But not her home. She'd sheltered here for long enough. It was time to face the world again.

She knew she could. She'd schooled herself to be independent.

So why was the thought of Jake Hunter walking away so disturbing?

'So what's the story with Tori?' he asked Rob.

It was after dark. There were only two guests staying at Manwillinbah Lodge right now, and both had gone to bed early. Rob had organised a theatre night—an old showing of *Casablanca*. He'd set up a themed dinner, decorated the sitting room with black-and-white posters, even worn a hat— but both his guests were weary and just wanted their own beds.

They were fire victims, too, Jake had discovered. Both were elderly women, living in temporary accommodation, organising to rebuild. They'd come here for time out, because the process was leaving them exhausted, and all they wanted to do was sleep.

It left Rob dissatisfied, though. He loved being the entertainer, but by eight he was left to entertain himself and his boss. They sat on the back porch and watched the stars and drank beer—and Jake pushed.

'Tori,' he prodded again. 'Tell me about her.'

'I don't even know her.'

'But Barb's told you.'

'Nope. There're tragedies everywhere and if you're not told you don't ask. Some people need to talk about it, some people can't. All I know is that she was put in charge of the wildlife rescue effort and she was vet up on the ridge before the fires. I didn't know she was staying on-site but I did say they could use it for whatever they wanted. I told you that when I phoned.'

He had. There'd been a couple of days when the news

coming through from Australia was dreadful. He'd been ready to promise anything.

He still was.

'I don't want to kick Tori out,' he said now, uneasily. 'If she still wants to live there…'

'She doesn't. Barb says as soon as the last animal goes, so will she. It's fine to put it on the market.'

'Does she have somewhere to go?'

'I have no idea,' Rob said, giving him a curious glance. 'I've never met the lady until last night, and five minutes with her didn't give me much time for in-depth questions. Yours was worse—how many questions did you manage in your minute and a half?'

'Don't rub it in,' Jake growled. 'I don't make a great speed dater.'

'I don't think you make an anything dater,' Rob said, pouring another beer. 'But you've met the lady properly today. What's she like?'

'Smart. Tired. Worried.' And very cute, he thought, but he didn't say it. Really sexy, despite those appalling clothes.

'Tired and worried equals everyone up here in the hills,' Rob said, not hearing his afterthoughts. 'So we're back to smart. How smart?'

'She's a vet.'

'And?'

'And she had the gumption to walk away from me when I was being an—'

'I know exactly what you were being,' Rob said, and had the temerity to grin. 'Good for Tori.'

'She practically told me to leave today, too.'

'You're kidding. It's your property.'

'Which she's legally entitled to be on. Oh, she wasn't rude. She evicted me in the most businesslike way. Maybe she's a man hater.'

'Not if she agreed to dating. So you're interested?'

'I'm not interested. I'm just concerned. Where has everyone else gone whose houses burned?'

'Relatives, friends, or there's a whole town of mobile homes—relocatables—set up further down the valley for anyone who needs them. You'll have passed them on your way from the airport.'

'She'll go there?'

'Why don't you ask her?'

'It's none of my business.'

'So why do you want to know?'

He didn't have an answer. He sat on, staring into the night, and finally Rob left him to his silence.

Leaving Jake alone with half a bottle of beer, a starlit sky and a silence so immense it was enough to take his breath away.

A faint rustle came from beside him. A wallaby was watching from the edge of the garden, moonlight glinting on its silvery fur.

'Hi,' Jake said, but the wallaby took fright and disappeared into the shadows. Leaving Jake alone again.

He should go inside. He had journals to study. He didn't do…nothing.

But the stars were immense, and somewhere under them, alone up on the mountain, was Tori.

A woman with shadows?

She was nothing to do with him. So why did a faint, insistent murmur in his head tell him that she was?

CHAPTER THREE

He arrived at the farmhouse at nine the next morning and nobody answered the door.

He knocked three times. The same van he'd seen yesterday was in the driveway but there were no sounds coming from the house. There was no dog on the settee.

He tried the door and it opened, unlocked and undefended. 'Hi, Tori,' he called. 'It's Jake.'

Still no answer.

She'd been expecting him.

Should he come back later? He hesitated and then thought maybe she was in the surgery again, doing something that couldn't be interrupted. He went through cautiously—and stopped at the open door.

Even from here he could tell the koala was dead. The little animal was facing him, curled on her side, still. The cage door was open.

He crossed to the cage and stooped, putting his hand on her fur to make sure. But yes, she was gone. Simply, he thought. There was no sign of distress. The IV lines Tori had attached yesterday had been removed but were lying neatly to the side, as if they'd been removed after death.

She looked as if she'd hardly moved since yesterday.

She'd simply died.

He'd had patients who'd done this—just died. The operation had been a success, yet the assault on their bodies had been too great, their hearts had simply stopped.

Mostly it happened in the aged, where maybe there'd been a question of whether the operation should have been done at all, only how could you convince a patient that you couldn't remove cancer because there was a risk of heart failure? Maybe you tried, but the patient could elect to have the operation anyway.

He hated cases like those. He hated this.

He knelt and saw, closer now and more dreadfully, the full extent of scar tissue. He thought about what this little animal must have gone through in the past six months and he knew that yesterday's decision to operate must have been a hard one for Tori to make.

Where was she?

He glanced around, out through the window, and then he saw her. She was out at the edge of the clearing, and he knew what she was doing.

Hadn't she cried enough?

She didn't get attached to her patients. She couldn't. Getting attached was the way of madness.

She was crying so hard she could barely see the ground she was trying to dig.

This was the first of the animals she'd tried to bury. Up until now there'd been volunteers taking away bodies of the animals she'd failed.

This was the end. Her last failure. If she'd known it would turn out like this she'd have euthanised her six months ago.

She'd had to make a decision. She'd got it wrong, and there were no volunteers left to bury her.

So much loss. So much appalling waste. Dad, Micki, one tiny baby with no life at all…

One little koala who somehow represented them all.

'I can't do this any more,' she whispered and hit the ground with the spade. The spade shuddered back. Was she hitting tree roots?

She swore and hit the ground again. Three spade lengths away, Rusty flinched, as if the little dog felt every shudder.

'You and me both,' she told Rusty and shoved the spade uselessly down again. This was dumb, dumb, dumb, but she did not want to take the little koala's body down the mountain to the veterinary crematorium. *She did not.*

All she could see was the Combadeen cemetery, two graves with brass headstones. Dad. Micki. Micki's with a tiny extra plaque, white on silver.

No.

She shoved the spade down hard again, uselessly. She gulped back tears—and suddenly the spade was taken out of her hands.

Where he came from she didn't know. She knew nothing, only that the spade was tossed aside, two strong arms enfolded her and held her close. And let her sob.

He'd never held a woman like this. He'd never felt emotion like this.

Jake was chief anaesthetist in a specialist teaching hospital in Manhattan. Once upon a time he'd spent time with patients, but that seemed long since. Now he handled only critical cases. Patient interviews and examinations were done by his juniors. His personal contact with patients was confined to reassurance as they slipped under anaesthetic, and occasional further reassurance as they regained consciousness.

If there were problems during an operation, it was mostly the surgeon who talked to the family. As anaesthetist Jake took no risks. He did his job and he did it well. There were seldom times he needed to talk. Now, as he faced Tori's real and dreadful grief, he realised he actively kept away from this type of anguish.

His mother had cried at him all of his life. He'd done with tears.

And this was just a koala.

Just a koala. Even as he thought it, he recalled the limp little body lying alone down at the house, the scar tissue, the evidence of a six-month battle now lost. He looked around him and saw the blackened skeletons of a ravaged forest. His mother had cried for crying's sake. He knew instinctively that Tori's tears were very different.

So much death…

Tori was trying desperately to pull herself together, sniffing against his shirt, tugging back. 'I'm sorry,' she managed. 'This is stupid. It was a risk, operating on her. I should have put her down. I should have…'

'You weren't to know what you should or shouldn't have done,' he said gently. 'You did your best. That's all anyone can ask.'

'No, but she was wild. She's been through so much.'

'You didn't add to that. Tori, you had to give her every chance.'

'But was I operating for me?' she demanded, sounding desperate. She'd managed to pull back now and was wiping her hand furiously across her cheeks. 'I named her! How stupid was that?'

'You told me you didn't.'

'I told everyone I didn't. All the volunteers I've worked with. The nurses. The drivers. The firefighters who brought animals in. I told them we can't afford to get attached. There are so many. If we get attached we'll go crazy. Let's do our best for every individual animal and let's stay dispassionate.'

There was nothing dispassionate about Tori. She looked

wild. Her face was blotched from weeping. The spade she was working with was covered with ashes and dirt. Her hands were filthy and she'd wiped her hands across her sodden face.

She looked like someone who'd just emerged from this burned-out forest—a fire victim herself—and something inside him felt her pain. Or felt more than that. It hurt that she was hurting, and it hurt a lot.

He wanted to hug her again—badly—but she was past hugging. She had her arms folded across her breasts in an age-old gesture of defence. Trying to stop an agony that was unstoppable?

This was much more than the death of one koala, he thought, as bad as that was. There were levels to this pain that he couldn't begin to understand.

'Keep yourself to yourself.' His mother's words sounded through the years. 'Don't get involved—you'll only get hurt.'

Wise advice? He'd always thought so, but right now it was advice he was planning to ignore.

'What did you call her?' he asked, and she hiccupped on a sob and tried to glare at him. It didn't come off. How could it?

'Manya'

Why was she glaring? Did she think he'd mock?

Maybe she did. He knew instinctively that Tori was assessing him and withdrawing. As if he'd think she was stupid—when stupid was the last thing he'd think her.

'Why Manya?' he asked, searching for the right words to break through. 'What does it mean?'

'Just…"little one." It's from the language of the native people from around here. Not that it matters. It was only… I talked to her.' She sounded desperate again, and totally bewildered. 'I had to call her something. I had to talk to her.'

'I guess you did,' he said. And then, as she still seemed to be drawing in on herself, he thought maybe he *could* make this professional. Maybe it'd make it easier. 'Do you know why she died?'

'No.' She spread her filthy hands and stared down at them, as if they could give her some clue. She shook her head. 'Or maybe I do. She's been under stress for months but I thought we were winning. I knew she wouldn't be able to go back to the wild, but there are sanctuaries that'd take her, good places that'd seem like freedom. And she was so close. But one tiny abscess… It must have been the last straw. She was fine when I checked on her at seven, and when I checked at eight she was dead. Everything just…stopped.'

'It does happen,' he said softly. 'To people, too.'

'Have you had it happen to patients?' she managed, and he knew she was struggling hard to sound normal. Her little dog nosed forwards and she picked him up and held him against her, shield-like. He licked her nose and she held him harder.

The dog was missing a leg, he saw with a shock, and his initial impression of him as an old dog changed. Not old. Wounded.

As Tori was wounded.

Have you had it happen to patients? Tori's question was still out there, and maybe talking medicine was the way to go until she had herself together.

'Not often,' he told her, 'but yes, I have. That it hasn't happened often means I've been lucky.'

'As opposed to me,' she said grimly. 'I've lost countless patients in the past six months.'

She looked exhausted to the point of collapse, he thought. Had she slept at all last night?

When had she last slept?

'Your patients are wild creatures,' he said, and he felt as if he was picking his way through a minefield, knowing it was important that she talk this out, but suspecting she could close up at any minute. 'My patients are the moneyed residents of Manhattan. There's no way a rich, private hospital will cause them stress, and there's the difference.' He hesitated. 'Tori, let me dig for you.'

'I can do it.' She put the little dog down and grabbed the spade again.

'Can you?'

She closed her eyes, gave herself a minute and then opened them. 'No. This is dumb. I accept that now. The ground's one huge root ball. I'll take her down the mountain and get her cremated.'

'But you don't want to.'

'Just…just because I named her,' she whispered, hugging the spade, while the little dog nosed her boots in worry. 'I wanted her buried here. At least the edges of the bush here are still alive. I wanted her buried under living trees. Does that make sense?'

'It does,' he said, strongly and surely, and before she could protest again, he took the spade from her hands and started digging.

She was right. The ground was so hard it would be more sensible to cremate her. Only there was something about Tori that said this burial was deeply important on all sorts of levels. So he put all his weight behind the spade and it slid a couple of inches in. Slowly he got through the hardened crust to the root-filled clay below, while Tori watched on in silence.

After a couple of minutes she sank to her knees and gathered the little dog against her.

'What's his name?' he asked, trying not to sound like the digging was as hard as it was.

'Rusty.'

'How did he lose his leg?'

'Fire,' she said harshly, and he glanced at the little dog in surprise. He'd lost his leg but he wasn't otherwise scarred.

'He was burned?'

'Wasn't everything around here?' She hugged him closer and got another nose lick for her pains. 'But Rusty was lucky—sort of. He was… I found him in the fireplace of…of where I lived. Over there.' She motioned to the neighbouring property. 'Part of the bricks had collapsed, trapping his leg, but otherwise he was okay. He was my dad's Rusty. He's just waiting 'til he comes home.'

Her voice broke. No more questions were allowed, Jake thought, while she struggled for control, so he kept right on digging.

It took time. Ten minutes. Fifteen. He wasn't in a hurry. This was giving Tori time to catch her breath, figure if she wanted to tell him more.

There were cockatoos screeching in the gums about his head. Apart from the birds and the sound of the spade against the earth, there was nothing but silence.

What had happened to this woman? He shouldn't ask, but finally he had to.

'So who did you lose?' he asked into the silence, and for a while he thought she wouldn't answer.

Then, 'My father and my sister,' she said flatly, dreadfully. 'My sister was eight months pregnant.'

Dear God, he thought helplessly. Where to take this from here? 'You all lived over there?' he tried.

'We did. Micki… Margaret… My sister's relationship had fallen apart and she'd come home, so she could have her baby with us. Toby and I were going to look after her for the first few weeks after the birth.' She took a deep breath. 'But then they died. Dad and Micki and Benedict. Benedict was Micki's baby. A little boy. She was going to call him Benedict. I found Rusty three days later when I finally got back up here, but there was nothing else left. Nothing.'

It took his breath away. He felt ill. But desperately he wanted to help, and somehow he knew that the only way to do that was to keep on going. Keep digging—and keep on talking.

'So...Toby?'

'Toby was my fiancé.'

'But he wasn't killed?'

'What do you think?' She laughed, mirthlessly, and buried her face in her dog's soft fur. Her laugh sounded close to hysteria.

He let her be for a moment, pushing the spade deeper into the tree roots. The grave was deep enough, but he knew instinctively that if he stopped, then so would she. She'd get back to the business of living—but maybe talking about the dying would help?

He'd done a bit of psychology in medical school but he'd never practised it. Now, however, what to do seemed to be instinctive. A human skill rather than a professional one? Whatever, it seemed to be working.

'Sorry,' she said at last, sniffing and giving Rusty a bit of slack. 'That...that sounds dumb. Of course you'd think he'd be killed. But Toby...well, Toby was a charmer, and he was also a survivor. He was a lovely, vibrant guy, a photographer who came up here last autumn and took pictures of the mountains, took pictures of my vet clinic—and finally stayed.'

She paused again but then went on, more in control now. 'I need to tell you... Dad started the vet practice up here when Micki and I were kids. Mum died early but Dad looked after us really well. We had a great childhood. Micki married and moved interstate—I did veterinary science. Then Dad was diagnosed with multiple sclerosis. The past couple of years have been hard. But then along came Toby and he made us both laugh. He brought the house to life, and when he asked me to marry him I don't know who was happier, me or Dad. Toby didn't have any money, but what could be more natural than he stay here? His photography would take off, I'd do the vet work I love and we'd live happily ever after.'

He let that sink in for a bit, and dug a few more spadefuls. This was getting to be a very deep hole and still he didn't have the full story. 'But…' he prompted softly, and he thought she wouldn't answer but finally she did.

'So then Micki came home for Christmas because her relationship had ended. She was having a tough pregnancy but Toby charmed her as well. Maybe…maybe things between Toby and me weren't as good as they could have been but Micki and Dad loved him.'

'And then the fires hit.'

'Then the heat hit,' she said dully. 'Micki was so pregnant she could hardly move. Dad was having one of his bad spells. He could hardly move. On the day… It was so hot. There was no sign of fires, but I was nervous. Everyone was nervous. Then the district nurse rang to say she didn't want to come up the mountain because she was scared her car might boil. But Dad had run out of his medication. So I made a run down into the valley. I'd only be away for an hour or so. Toby was here with the other car. What could go wrong? And then the fires hit.'

'There's no need…' he said, hearing the raw anguish in her voice and not wanting to make her say it. He'd stopped digging now. He moved towards her but she waved him back.

'Let me finish,' she whispered. 'He heard on the radio that there were fires on the other side of the ridge—that's where they started. So Toby took the van and went to see. He took magnificent photographs. You probably saw them—they were the ones beamed around the world the next day, after the wind changed and over a hundred people were killed, and Dad and Micki and Benedict and all the animals in our vet clinic were left without a vehicle to escape in. Dad put Rusty in the fireplace and protected him with his body. Our three big dogs—Mutsy and Pogo and Bandit, they died, too. One little dog was all they could save.'

Once more he made a move to go to her, but she flinched. She swiped her hand across her face again and she sniffed. Trying desperately to move on. 'Enough,' she said bleakly. 'Toby made a fortune, and I lost everything. I promised Micki she'd be safe here, but it didn't happen. I failed her as I failed…so many. Trusting Toby. Leaving the mountain. But it's dopey to keep crying. We'll bury Manya, and then Rusty and I will move on.

'Where?'

'I don't know,' she whispered. 'This is where I belong but I don't know any more. Look, it's deep enough. I can do the rest.'

'You'll do nothing,' he growled. 'I'm the undertaker, today. Stay.'

He helped Tori gather sheaths of fresh eucalyptus leaves. He carried the little body from the house. They laid her on a bed of the leaves she'd loved, they covered her with more leaves and then he filled in the grave. They spread more leaves on the freshly dug earth, and then Jake stood back, silent, not knowing where to go next.

Not knowing how to help.

He wanted to hold her again, but Tori was standing apart, rigid, as if ashamed at her previous show of emotion.

'Thank you,' she whispered. 'Thank you so much. I… When do you want your house back?'

'Let's look at it now,' he said and held out his hand. She looked at it but she didn't take it. Her reserve was back again. The woman who'd sobbed her heart out was well hidden.

'Of course,' she said, stiffly, and led the way back down to the house, with Rusty limping along behind them. She ushered him into one room after another, letting him see it all.

Apart from yesterday he'd never been in this house. When

his father died it had already been let to tenants who'd wanted to keep renting. A realtor had acted as intermediary, and there'd been no opportunity or need for him to see it.

The grand old homestead was battered now, from years of renting, from six months of being used as an animal hospital and from the fires themselves. The building hadn't burned but it was still smoke stained and grim. The only furniture was what they'd needed for the animal hospital.

The last room Tori showed him was what was obviously the master bedroom. He stood at the door and saw how she'd been living for the past six months, and he drew in his breath in dismay.

There was a camp stretcher in the corner. There were half a dozen cardboard cartons acting as storage and as a bedside table. A basket lay in the corner for Rusty.

Nothing else.

At speed dating he'd thought she'd looked dowdy. It was a miracle she'd managed to look presentable at all.

'No mirror?' he asked, trying to make it sound as though he was joking.

'No mirror.' She'd recovered a little now; her voice was firmer. Moving on. 'Just as well, as I suspect I'd scare myself silly.'

'You look all right to me.'

'Said the man who looked at me like I was a porrywiggle on our five-minute date.'

'A what?'

'A tadpole. Something that wiggles out of pond scum.'

'I never said…'

'You never had to. Have you seen enough?'

'More than enough. Are these all your possessions?'

'I live light,' she said, in a tight voice. 'I can be gone in half an hour.'

'Where are you staying tonight?'

'You're not kicking me out tonight?' she demanded, alarmed, and he shook his head.

'I'm not kicking you out at all. I'm asking if you have an alternative—something a bit less appalling than here.'

'Here's fine.'

'Here's not fine. This place needs an army to make it habitable.'

'It's a lovely house.'

'It could be a lovely house. It's anything but now. Do you have anywhere you can go?'

'Of course I do,' she retorted, but he thought that she was lying.

There were all sorts of emotions twisting inside him right now. He didn't want to get involved—when had he ever?— but walking away from her...

He'd be as bad as Toby if he left her anchored to this place, to her grief, to her loss.

'Come down to Manwillinbah Lodge,' he found himself saying. 'You know the lodge?'

'I know it, but...'

'But what?'

'I can't.'

'Why not?'

'It's your place.'

'It's a guesthouse and it's almost empty. So I'm offering, and I believe you'd be sensible to accept.' He spread his hands. 'Tori, either you stay here tonight in this bleak and lonely place and, I suspect, cry your eyes out again for a little koala called Manya, or you come down the mountain and let Rob take care of you while you regroup.' Then, as she hesitated, he added, 'You know, you'd be doing Rob a favour. He loves the lodge being full and he loves company. Since the fire, all his guests have come and stared out into the night and not wanted to talk.'

'I don't think I want to talk.'

'No, but our housekeeper can cook for you, and Rob can make you smile. Rob's good with people.'

She looked at him curiously at that. 'You talk as if you mean you're not.'

'I'm not a people person.'

'Yet you let me soak your shirt.'

'Sometimes I'm compelled to be a people person.'

'That sounds like your five-minute date. Like you want to be out of here.'

'I didn't mean it to sound like that,' he said, flinching. Hell, he had to figure out how to sound nice.

But to his relief she was smiling, a faint smile but a smile nonetheless. 'Yeah, okay, you're not a people person but you did very well just now,' she said. 'I was really grateful for your shirt and you held on manfully. So whether you wanted to bolt or not, the fact is you didn't and I'm not asking questions.' She turned and looked down at her camp bed, at the detritus of six months' camping in this sooty, makeshift home. He could see her indecision.

'You don't really want to stay here.'

'I have Rusty.' Though Rusty was on the verandah again, staring fixedly at the road. Still endlessly waiting.

'Rusty can come with you. Stay in the lodge while you figure where to go.'

She stared down at the camp stretcher again. 'I've been offered a job,' she said. 'In a small-animal clinic down the mountain.'

'Will you take it?'

'I don't…I don't know.'

'When did you last sleep through the night?'

'I don't know that either,' she admitted, and people person or not, he took her hands in his and held.

'Tori, you're in no state to decide anything. Come to the lodge. Let Rob look after you for a month or so.'

'A month? No.'

'Okay, come for tonight and take it from there,' he said hastily. 'But you need to sleep and you need to start thinking of something other than destruction.'

'That's what Barb said when she talked me into five-minute dating,' she whispered. 'I need to move on. It doesn't work. How can it?'

'Yeah, well, maybe the dating wasn't a great idea for either of us,' he said ruefully. 'Let's try it another way.'

'Do you need to move on, too?'

'No,' he said blankly. 'I meant you.'

She looked up at him then, and another glimmer of a smile crossed her face. 'Really? It's only me who's got ghosts? Why do I get the feeling you're as strained as I am?'

'I'm not.'

'Okay.' She pulled her hands away and held them up in sur-render. 'You're staying at the lodge as well?'

'Until Monday.'

'You think you can stand my company?'

'Of course I can.'

'There's no "of course" about it,' she said, still with a touch of humour. 'One and a half minutes, as I remember.'

'It was you who walked out.'

'So it was,' she said, and suddenly her smile became real. 'And I can do it again if life gets tricky. But now… Does the lodge have baths?'

'There's a spa in every room.'

'A spa,' she said, awed.

'And a heated swimming pool. And beds with so many down-filled pillows you can't count them. One of Rob's ditzy blondes did his decorating for him, and I have to say she can't have been as ditzy as most.'

'Ditzy?'

'Rob thinks ditzy equals sexy.'

'And you don't?'

'Um, no.'

'Well, I'm not even going to go there,' she said and her smile was still in place. 'I can't imagine what woman would have tied you to speed dating for more than five minutes. But look, I need to clear up here. If Rob agrees to having Rusty and me…'

'Of course he'll agree. I'm the owner.'

'He's the manager. I'll phone and check,' she said, with a touch of reproof. 'And I'm paying. Let's make this formal.'

'You will not pay.'

'I'll pay or I won't come,' she said with asperity. 'And don't look at me like that. I've spent almost nothing in six months, and I'm tired of charity. I know that sounds ungrateful,' she said, suddenly rueful, 'but there it is. I'll phone him, I'll lock up and I'll come down later this afternoon.'

He was being dismissed?

'Can I help clean up?'

'No,' she said. 'Thank you, Dr. Hunter.'

'Jake,' he growled. 'And don't be pig-headed. I *will* help you.'

'Jake, she said, but still with a touch of formality. 'And pig-headed or not, I'd like to clean up by myself.'

And suddenly he could see her hidden agenda. He could take offence at her knocking back his help—or he could understand.

This place was filled with six months' memories. She needed to say goodbye on her own terms.

She might well cry again. The thought was bad but he suspected she needed to, and she certainly had the right.

How could he ever have thought her frumpy? How could he ever have thought she was uninteresting?

He gazed down into her troubled face and he thought suddenly, I'd like to hold her again. And then he thought…

I'd really like to kiss her. It wasn't sympathy now. She had so many levels. She was such a woman…

He couldn't kiss her. Of course he couldn't; she'd run a mile and the thought was totally illogical.

And besides, he thought, trying hard for logical, she was too dirty, too tear-stained, too *not the sort of woman he kissed*.

But as she turned away, as she knelt to start filling boxes, he looked down at her, in her tight, faded jeans clinging to her neat figure like a second skin, at her torn T-shirt, at the way a curl was wisping down the nape of her neck…and he was aware of a sharp stab of missed opportunity.

What would she be like to kiss?

He didn't know, and he had no business thinking about finding out. He formed relationships with women who knew the rules—independent women who wanted nothing but a lighthearted relationship which went nowhere.

Would Tori understand those rules? He knew she wouldn't, and there was no way he was risking giving pain.

So he wanted to kiss her but he couldn't. She didn't even want his help cleaning this house—and he had to respect her wishes.

'I'll see you down at the lodge,' he said, more harshly than he intended. 'Before dinner?'

'See you then,' she said without looking up. 'Thank you, again, Jake.'

So that was that. He turned and left, leaving Tori shoving welfare clothes into welfare boxes. Packing up life as she knew it—and moving on.

While a little dog watched Jake's car until it disappeared from view.

The place was a mess. She gazed around the house and thought she couldn't just walk out. It wasn't fair.

She should have let Jake help, and maybe if it hadn't been Jake she would have. But then Jake wasn't anyone else. The man had her thoroughly off balance. The equilibrium she'd striven so hard to reach had been tossed off course by the death of one little koala—and then by the way she'd reacted to Jake.

For this was more than grief.

Barb said she had to move on. Her head told her she couldn't, but her body was telling her it was more than time.

So she'd thought he was lovely and she'd sobbed all over him. What a turn-on. She headed into the bathroom to fetch her toiletries. Despite what she'd told Jake there was a mirror there, and she saw what she looked like. A nightmare.

'Just forget it,' she said fiercely to a pile of second-hand clothes she had no use for. 'Your body would react to anything in pants right now. You're needy and weepy and pathetic. So get a grip and don't even begin to think that Jake Hunter's seeing you as anything more than a basket case.'

She sniffed.

'And don't go blubbering about that as well,' she snapped to her reflection, and headed back to the bedroom and kicked the closest cardboard box, which promptly collapsed. She stared at it as if it'd personally betrayed her—and then the phone rang.

'Doc Nicholls?'

'Yes.'

'It's Combadeen Cleaners,' a woman's voice said. 'We've been paid to clean the place you're using up on the ridge. Cart away garbage. Give stuff to welfare. Scrub. Do whatever you want.'

'You've been paid?' she said cautiously.

'This guy—Jake Hunter?—apparently he owns the lodge as well as your place? He said you're moving out. If it's okay with you, he said you do what you want, then leave the rest for us. When you're finished, leave a key on the kitchen table. We'll collect it tonight. We'll clean and lock up after ourselves. But it's only if you want us. He made that clear. We've been paid already but it's up to you.'

It's up to you. Jake understood. He was helping, but on her terms. The offer took her breath away.

For the past six months she'd been in charge. She'd been giving instructions. She'd organised.

Jake had listened to what she'd said, but he'd heard the underlying message and he'd organised around her.

The woman was giving her time to think about it. She gazed around her, at six months' chaos of a house being used as an animal hospital.

She should do it herself.

Jake was bossy, she thought. He was autocratic. He also scared her, just a little, the way he understood.

Logic said she should stay right away from Jake Hunter and his grandiose gestures.

It wasn't going to happen. She sniffed again and thought if she cried one more time today she'd need an IV line to replace fluids.

'Thank you,' she said simply. 'I accept with pleasure.'

Would she come?

Jake paced the lodge and thought he should have been more insistent.

Why was it so important she accept?

He didn't know. He only knew that it was.

CHAPTER FOUR

SHE'D done what she could. The cleaners could deal with the rest. Tori sat in her little white van with Rusty close beside her, and thought leaving wasn't as easy as it sounded.

Stupid or not, it was a grief in itself. Moving away from the ridge…

She and Rusty had spent the first dreadful nights after the fire on Barb's couch. Then, when they'd found Jake's place and settled that it could be a staging post for injured wildlife, it had seemed sensible that she move in here. Six months later she was still not looking further than her next patient. Until now.

Rusty was staring out the window with longing, along the road that led to her burned-out home.

Home.

She closed her eyes. It didn't help to be angry—she knew that—but the rage she felt towards Toby was still real and dreadful. That she could have imagined she loved him… He hadn't come near her since the fire, which was just as well. He was a coward of the worst kind—and she'd thought she'd loved him.

So don't trust your stupid heart again, she told herself. Move on from the ridge but do not trust.

She was trying to get her tired mind to think.

Maybe accepting Jake's invitation for accommodation at the lodge was a mistake, she decided. But staying up here tonight in the empty refuge seemed unthinkable, and landing on Barb again was equally impossible. There were relocatable homes set up down in the valley for anyone displaced by the fires. She could move into one of those.

But not tonight, she thought. She'd give herself this night of respite.

A night with Jake?

No.

This was a night at a lovely guesthouse, she told herself fiercely. It had nothing to do with Jake. It was a night of in-dulgence before moving onto practicalities. To the dreary other side…

She glanced at Rusty, sitting passively beside the card-board box that held all her worldly possessions, the practical things—changes of clothes, toiletries, things she'd had to find to survive.

She would survive. She and Rusty.

'And we'll come back to the ridge,' she told the little dog as he looked mournfully along the road towards where they used to live. 'Dad and Micki and Benedict, and Mutsy and Pogo and Bandit—they're still here. Just a little bit, but they're still here.'

But for now they had to leave.

'We'll come back,' she said again, and she flicked the engine into life and drove out the gate—and to Rusty's great sorrow she turned right instead of left, down into the valley instead of where they'd left so much. 'I promise you, Rusty. We'll come home.'

She was coming. She rang Rob and it was all Jake could do not to listen in on the extension.

'You're really worried about her,' Rob said when he finished.

'She's had a tough time.'

'So has half this valley.'

'I don't know half this valley,' he growled. 'I know Tori.'

'Only since yesterday... Right,' Rob said thoughtfully. 'So shall we give her the honeymoon suite?'

'What?'

'The best,' Rob said patiently. 'The one I tried to put you in. It's expensive.'

'Yes, but charge her half-rates.'

'You don't want to give it to her free?'

'If we don't charge her, then she won't come.'

'And you want her to come.'

'Yes,' he snapped, and Rob grinned.

'I see,' he said thoughtfully. 'Shall I ring Barb, then, and tell her the five-minute dating was a success?'

'Just try it.'

'That's what I thought,' Rob said. 'Okay, not yet. But I'm thinking I might get Mrs. Matheson to pull out all the stops. It's time we had a great dinner.'

'Nothing special,' Jake said.

'You don't want to scare her?'

'Rob…'

'I know,' his manager said, placating. 'But I'm thinking lobster. She can think we have it every night, because we're not trying to impress her at all.'

'Manwillinbah Lodge.'

She turned into the driveway and she could scarcely believe she was on the same planet as the place she'd just left. The lodge looked gracious and inviting, long and low and sprawling. Beyond rambling rose gardens were acres of grapevines, just coming into bud. It looked not where she belonged at all.

Why was she panicking?

She shouldn't be here. She should be somewhere she could be alone to think things through. Though hadn't she had enough time to think things through, and where had that got her?

But before her muddled thoughts could take her any further, her car door was tugged open, and Jake was looking in.

'Hey,' he said softly. 'I was starting to think I'd need to come up the mountain and fetch you. Welcome, Tori. Welcome, Rusty.'

He was smiling. That smile was enough to make a girl panic all on its own. 'I was just coming to tell you…to tell Rob I wasn't coming,' she muttered. 'And to thank you for the cleaners.'

He nodded, suppressing his smile. 'That makes sense. Or not. The cleaners were my pleasure. As for not staying… You want to have dinner while you tell us why not?'

'I can't stay here,' she said wildly, gesturing towards the house.

'Why ever not?'

'I don't fit.'

'You fit in fine,' he said. 'Our only two guests were burned out themselves. They're here to sleep.'

'I don't have any clothes.'

'Odd,' he said thoughtfully. 'You'd have thought I'd have noticed no clothes.'

'You know what I mean.'

He did. His gaze met hers and she knew he understood. 'You look great,' he said softly. 'Tori, you look lovely. Jeans and T-shirt are practically uniform here and no one's going to judge you even if they weren't. Dinner's on the table in an hour. That gives you time to have a bath first.'

'You're saying I'm dirty?'

'I'm saying there's a heated spa bath on your balcony with a view to die for. It's totally private. If you're dirty to start with, there's only you to notice. Unless you want me to come scrub your back?'

'No!'

'No?' He was laughing now, and suddenly she found herself smiling back. Okay, she thought, maybe this wouldn't be as bad as it seemed. She didn't need to trust. She only needed to stay for a night. And tomorrow…

'Worry about right now,' Jake said gently and, chameleon-like, his laughter was gone again. It was replaced by a gentle concern she found disconcerting.

Insidious. Impossible to resist.

Inviting her to trust. Terrifying.

'Okay, no back-scrubbing,' he said, and he put out a hand to help her from the car. 'Nothing but bath, food, sleep, and if that's not what you need I'll eat my medical degrees. There's no pressure, Tori. You're our welcome guest.'

His hand was waiting. Just waiting. All she had to do was accept.

'I won't bite,' he said softly. 'Rob's in the house, as is our housekeeper, Mrs. Matheson. There are two elderly ladies lying on Rob's fabulous lounges on the balcony watching the cockatoos. One's wearing dungarees, one's wearing tweed. Life's safe here, Tori. It's a refuge, if you like. You provided refuge for your battered wild creatures. Now it's time for you to take refuge.'

'I don't need—'

'I think you do. Barb thinks you do, too.' He hesitated but then continued. 'Maybe I should confess I phoned Barb this afternoon. When she heard your koala was dead she was all for rushing up the mountain and taking you home herself. Only I gather Barb has a husband, five sons and a menagerie. We both thought you'd be best here. So what's it to be, Tori? Here, or Barb's, because no one's going to let you stay in a motel by yourself tonight.'

'Even if I want to?'

'If you really want, then we'll pay for a five-star hotel in the best part of Melbourne,' he said. 'And you needn't think I'd have to personally pay—according to Barb half the valley would have their hands in their pockets in a minute to help you. So what's it to be?'

Still his hand was held out to her.

What was it to be?

She could still drive away. She knew she could.

There was a bath inside. A bath!

And Jake.

There was the problem.

She looked up at him. He smiled.

She couldn't trust.

She didn't need to trust. This was a night in a guesthouse, nothing more.

She took a deep breath. She tried to smile back. She put her hand in his and let him pull her up.

The tug had her rising too fast. She almost overbalanced, but he had her steady, catching her shoulders, holding.

He was so near.

She should pull away—but didn't.

'Tori...' he said uncertainly, and she just looked at him. Sex on legs, she thought absently.

No. He was much, much more.

Get a grip, she thought frantically and shoved her hands up, breaking his grip. She came close to falling back down into the car—but didn't. Thankfully. A girl had some pride.

'I... Thank you,' she muttered and managed to get herself round to the other side of the car to retrieve her cardboard box.

'I like your luggage,' he said, and grinned.

'Eat your heart out, Mr. Gucci,' she said, managing a smile in return. 'This is so next year's catwalk.'

'I believe it is,' he said. 'If there's anyone who can start a trend it would be you.'

'Enough with the compliments,' she said, feeling…disconcerted. No, more than that, totally flummoxed. 'You promised me a bath.'

'I did. Let me carry your box.'

'I can manage myself,' she said with an attempt at dignity. 'Once upon a time I depended on others. I don't do that any more.'

'It's only carrying a box,' he said mildly.

'No,' she said softly, as she carted her belongings up the steps and into the house. 'Believe me, it's much, much more.'

She lay back in the vast spa; she let the bubbles float up around her and she felt as if she was floating herself. From here she could see all the way across the valley floor. There were candles lit around her, gardenia with maybe a hint of citrus. The housekeeper had lit them as she'd settled her into the room.

'And don't worry about privacy,' she'd said. 'There's one-way glass so you can see forever but no one can see you, even if there was someone outside, which there isn't. The one-way glass is brilliant. Jake had it installed just after his father died.'

'Jake did that?'

'He wants this place to be the best. It was his stepmother's passion, and we want to carry it on.'

Jake's stepmother's passion… There was a lot here she didn't understand, that she hadn't thought through.

She knew this place had been built by the local doctor and his wife. Charlie McDonald had cared for this community for as long as most people remembered. He'd cared for her mother during her long illness, allowing her to die at home surrounded by her family and her beloved animals. Tori remembered him with deep affection, and with gratitude.

He'd lived in Combadeen and his wife had run the lodge. The place up on the ridge had been his weekend retreat, so they'd been weekend neighbours. But just after she'd started university he'd retired to the city, and she'd not heard of him until his funeral.

And now…

The old doctor was Charlie McDonald. Jake was Jake Hunter.

Illegitimate? Who knew with mixed families?

She tried to remember community gossip. There was talk of a son at his funeral. She remembered a faded baby photo on Dr. McDonald's surgery wall. That must be Jake.

She'd find out. She had all the time in the world to get it right, she thought dreamily as she sank deeper into bubbles. But then she thought, No, she was only here for a night until she organised something more permanent, and Jake himself would return to New York. There'd be no time for questions.

The thought left her curiously bereft.

But at least she could sleep tonight, she reminded herself. She glanced through into the bedroom, at the enormous bed piled with white-on-white eiderdowns and feather pillows. A woman could melt into a bed like this.

As opposed to melting into a man like Jake Hunter?

She was delirious. That was the only possible explanation for where her mind was taking her. She was *not* thinking of doing any melting into any man.

All she had to do to stop that was to think of Toby. Betrayal. A heartache that would never leave her.

Jake was different.

Maybe or maybe not, she thought sharply, but Jake was heading back to New York and he didn't want to even indulge in five-minute dating, much less anything else. She was tired beyond belief and her mind was playing tricks.

So get out of the bath, get to dinner, so you can go to bed.

Right. She wiggled even deeper under the bubbles.

'Tori?'

Uh-oh. Jake's voice brought her bolt upright. 'Tori, are you okay?'

'I'm fine,' she managed, feeling…discombobulated. She was covered in bubbles and she was bright pink. Had she locked the door? She didn't think so.

'Dinner's ready. I've fed Rusty, but do you want yours here or in the dining room?'

In here, she thought, but then maybe he had it with him. Maybe if she said the word the door would open.

'In the dining room,' she squeaked.

'You want a hand out of the bath?'

'No!'

She heard him chuckle. 'Hey, I'm a doctor, remember? I'm used to human bodies.'

'You're not *my* doctor, and you're not used to this one. Go away.'

'Yes, ma'am,' he said and there was silence—and she pulled herself awkwardly out of the bath and thought maybe, just maybe, she should have let him in.

Maybe she even wanted to.

Maybe she was losing her mind.

The meal was served on the terrace. Tori left Rusty on her bed, watching the door—of course—and made her way cautiously through the dining room and outside. And paused.

She could see the whole world.

The valley meandered downhill, following the ancient river path. Far in the distance she could see the faint, flickering lights of the city at dusk, but the foreground was simple, natural beauty.

The dusk wasn't so deep that she couldn't see vines around the house, lines and lines, reaching into the distance. Gum trees followed the river—massive eucalypts with wide, spreading branches. For Tori, who'd lived with blackened skeletons for so long, the sight was enough to make her gasp.

'We thought you might have gone down the drain.'

It was Jake, rising to greet her. As well as Jake there was Rob and two tiny, wrinkled women, smiling a welcome. One of the women had her arm in a sling. She looked pale and strained, and she held her arm as if it hurt. The other looked a little better but not much. Her forehead was badly scarred, and she was glancing nervously at her companion as if she was deeply worried about her. Fire victims both. Six months raw.

They were all six months raw.

'Do you need introductions?' Rob said easily, rising as well. She'd recognised the women but was given introductions anyway. 'Tori, you must know Miss Glenda Parling—postmistress to Combadeen until fifteen years ago. And Mrs. Doreen Ryde? Doreen's Glenda's sister. You've already met Mrs. Matheson, our own personal wizard-chef, and of course you know Jake. Sit down and wrap yourself round some of Mrs. Matheson's cooking.'

Jake was holding her chair for her. There was nothing for her to do but sink onto the lovely upholstery—and sink into the night.

Jake and Rob were chatting, drawing the elderly ladies out between them. They let her be, as if protecting her. The conversation had obviously been going on before she got there. She was free to take in her surroundings and the people around her. The lilt of soft music in the background. The fragrance of…more gardenias?

And then the food arrived.

For six months she'd been living on snacks on the run. Whatever Jake and Rob planned for this place, it was obvious snacks on the run were not on the menu.

For all her life afterwards she remembered that meal.

First there were tiny garfish with slivers of lemon and curls of melting butter, cooked to perfection and leaving her mouth exploding with flavours of the sea.

She'd barely finished when fingers of crusty toast arrived, spread thickly with a creamy trout pate, with caviar on the side. Around the plate were tiny tomatoes, shreds of lettuce and curls of shallots. How could a salad taste of sunshine when winter was barely over? The greenhouse at the edge of the balcony gave her the clue.

The night grew more dream-like. Jake was filling her wineglass with something white and cool and luscious. She was achingly conscious of his presence, but he didn't speak to her and she didn't speak to him. Conversation was happening around her but she felt as if she was in some sort of bubble, free to be her with no intrusion.

Then came the lobster, and it took her breath away. It had to have been caught this morning, she thought. She'd never tasted lobster like this. She glanced up and Jake was watching her, enjoying her enjoyment. She should think of something to say, but it was too wonderful and she left him to think what he liked and went back to cracking a claw.

Or trying to crack a claw. She was struggling. Then Jake leaned over and cracked it for her, expertly, as though he'd cracked a thousand claws in his life. He tugged the flesh free and held it out. She almost took it straight into her mouth—but what was she thinking? Somehow she pulled back, took it in her fingers and slid it into her mouth herself. Almost decorous, but not quite.

Jake smiled and she tried to smile back and felt…and felt…

She didn't know what she was feeling. She wasn't making any sense to herself.

Rob was at her elbow then, asking if she wanted her wine

refilled. She put her hand over her glass in a gesture of panic. Had she only had one glass? She felt dizzy. Or maybe *floating* was a better word.

They were eating by candlelight now. The night sky was full of stars and the moon was rising, vast and round. It was unseasonably warm, and the warmth was adding to her feeling that she'd been transported to another world.

Jake was watching her—she knew it—and that added to the floating sensation as well.

'You can't always eat like this,' she managed as the housekeeper put a parfait of raspberries and chocolate before her. Mmm.

'Jake said we were to pull out all the stops tonight,' Mrs. Matheson said.

'Though the food's wonderful all the time,' Glenda ventured. 'This place is fabulous. Doreen and I keep coming here, whenever we need time out, and it's like heaven. If only we could bring Pickles…'

'Pickles?'

'Our cat,' Glenda said, suddenly sad, and once again Tori noticed her wince as she moved her hand. 'He was very traumatised during the fires, but he's better now. We're all traumatised. We live in the relocatable village while we rebuild, but we both have health problems. When things get too much we put Pickles in the cattery and come here.'

'Why can't you bring him?' she asked, trying to focus on something other than the food, the night, Jake. Mrs. Matheson was setting down platters of frosted grapes and tiny chocolates, and Jake was watching her with an air of a genie producing his magic. She could reach out and touch him.…

No.

'We don't welcome animals here,' Rob was telling her.

'But Rusty…'

'Rusty's a special request from the owner,' Rob said, giving

Jake a rueful grin. 'Old Doc's wife was allergic to dog and cat hair. The no-pet rule seemed easiest so we've stuck with it.'

'Old Doc being your father?' she asked Jake, and he gave a curt nod as if he didn't want to go there.

But this was obviously news to Doreen and Glenda. Clearly no one had explained who Jake was until now— maybe there'd been no need. Maybe he hadn't even eaten with the guests until tonight. Now they looked astounded.

'You're Doc McDonald's son?' they gasped as one, and got another curt nod.

'Oh, my dear…' Doreen whispered, sounding awed. 'Your father? He was the most wonderful man. Oh, when our papa died nothing was too much trouble.' She hesitated then, looking puzzled. 'You're not… He and Hazel didn't…' And then her face cleared. 'I know. You're Diane's son.'

'That's right.' Jake's voice said, *Don't go there*, but Doreen had had a wonderful dinner and wonderful wine and she was past picking up subtleties.

'Oh, my dear, of course you are,' Doreen said. 'Thelma said you were at the funeral but no one believed her. But you're the little boy Doc lost. He broke his heart over you.'

'Not so much as you'd notice,' Jake snapped, clearly wanting to move on. 'I had no contact with my father from the time I was three. I heard from him only once after my mother took me back to the States, but I was a man by then and…well…even then he didn't seem keen to get to know me.'

'Well, that's nonsense,' Glenda snapped back, as if rising to bait. She clutched her hand and winced again, but a little pain wouldn't stop her defending a man she clearly idolised. 'I was postmistress in Combadeen for forty years and I can tell you that your father wrote to you every single week, from the day your mother took you away with that awful American.

Big fat letters, they were, crammed with everything he could think of. He posted them every Friday. And you know what? Nearly every one of them came back, marked returned to sender. But he still kept sending them. Then about twenty years ago, he went over to the States. "I'm going to find him, Glenda," he told me, but three months later he came back. He looked dreadful—and he hadn't seen you. Your mother wouldn't let him near. Oh, that woman...'

Glenda's cheeks were pink with indignation, anger building and building. 'Not that it's any of my business,' she said, 'but to hear you say there was no contact... It makes my blood boil that your mother wouldn't let him keep in touch. But then he met Hazel. Even then, he and Hazel couldn't have children and I know he missed you every day of his life.'

There was a deathly silence round the table. Jake looked as if he'd gone into shock, Tori thought. His face was a mixture of conflicting emotions. Maybe she should reach out and touch him. Maybe she could reassure him.

Maybe she should just keep out of what was clearly not her business.

'You said he met Hazel twenty years ago,' Jake said, tightly now, angry and disbelieving. 'Surely you meant thirty. Or more.'

'Oh, no, dear,' Glenda said. 'That was why they couldn't have children. Hazel was in her early forties when they met. Of course they hoped, but it didn't happen.'

'But my mother left because of my father's affair with this...Hazel.'

'No, dear, she left because of the American. His name was Chuck or something appalling, and his automobile broke down here and he had to stay until it was mended and then...well, off he went, with your mother. And you. Your father couldn't believe it. He loved her so much. Oh, but it was never going to work. Your mother hated the life as a wife of a country doctor. She hated the calls, the feeling of everyone knowing everyone, the community. She just hated…here.'

'Are you a doctor as well?' Finally Doreen spoke. Her eyes were alight with pleasure—and with something else.

'Yes.'

'Oh, my dear,' Doreen breathed. 'To think, Glenda, Doc's son coming home, and a doctor as well.' And then she looked uncertainly at her sister and then directly at Jake. 'If you really are his son, I don't suppose… You know, Glenda won't go and see a doctor. She broke her wrist dragging me out of the fire. Since she left hospital she won't go back, and I know it hurts her terribly. Do you think we could trouble you to look at it. Just to tell us what you think?'

'I'm not sure that I could help—and I don't have registration to practise in this country,' Jake said, sounding flummoxed.

'No, but you could give us advice.'

'I don't think I can.'

'If you're Old Doc's son you could try,' Doreen said, suddenly stern, and Tori remembered she'd been a schoolteacher. 'She's in such pain. She hasn't slept for weeks. It hurts and hurts, and she doesn't tell me but I know she lies awake night after night. She doesn't want to go to bed because the pain takes over again. I'm so worried about her I don't know what to do.' The sternness left her. She sniffed, and then she sniffed again and finally she hiccupped on a sob, while Glenda stared at her in horror, as if she'd been betrayed.

'Doreen, don't.'

'He's Old Doc's son. He'll help us. He even looks like his father.'

'I didn't know my father,' Jake said tightly. 'You should go back to see your own doctor.'

'They just give her sleeping pills,' Doreen retorted, gulping back more tears. 'Sleeping pills and those other blue things that stop it hurting for a little bit but then her stomach gets upset and she won't keep taking them. And the sleeping pills don't work. She can't go on like this. Neither of us can.' She touched her chest, a fleeting gesture that spoke volumes. 'It hurts us both. Please help us.'

'We have no right to ask,' Glenda said, sounding angry and distressed.

Glenda was right, Tori thought. They had no right to ask for professional help from this man. He wasn't even qualified to practise in Australia.

But then, Tori thought of the way he'd worked with Manya, of the skills he'd shown. And he was an anaesthetist, she thought. He'd know about pain management.

Maybe he could help.

And despite her absolute certainty that she should stay out of this, Tori found herself inexorably caught up in Doreen's plea.

'Glenda, Jake's my friend,' she said softly, ignoring Jake for the moment and concentrating on Glenda. 'He helped me try and save my koala. Doreen's right. You knew Jake's dad so you know him. Will you let him help? Jake, can you see if there's anything you can do?'

She caught the flare of shock on Jake's face—but she'd started now. There was no way she could back off.

'Jake's also an anaesthetist,' she told Glenda, firmly but softly. 'Pain relief is what he does. Isn't that right, Jake?'

'Yes.' He had no choice but to agree.

'We know you don't practise medicine in Australia,' she continued, inexorably hooking him and keeping him hooked. 'But if all Glenda's been offered is sleeping pills and little blue pills… Morphine?'

'Yes,' Glenda said hopelessly. 'But my arm's better. They put a plate in it, and screws. It's as good as they can get it.'

And then…

'Can I see?' Jake said, and it was as if the whole world held its breath. *Can I see*. Those three little words had the capacity to turn this desperate little scene around.

Glenda stared at him, wide-eyed, and Jake gazed right back, not speaking, giving her time to make up her mind. The room held its collective breath.

And then, very slowly, Glenda held out her arm, and Tori wondered if Jake knew just how much trust went into that gesture.

Glenda had been postmistress in the valley forever, and her independence was legendary. When her postboys called in sick Glenda had been known to get on a bike and deliver herself, often two or three mail runs in the one day. For her to accept help…

But it seemed she was. Jake was pulling his chair round the table so he could sit facing her. Gently he took her hand in his, and while Glenda submitted her arm for inspection, while Tori watched Glenda place her trust in him, the warmth around Tori's heart grew and grew.

She should be concentrating on Glenda. She was—sort of. But when he'd taken Glenda's hand in his, it was as if he'd taken her own.

I could be in huge trouble here, she told herself, feeling dazed. I need to leave, right now. If I stay longer…

But she couldn't leave now.

Jake was holding Glenda's hand lightly in his, watching Glenda's face intently. The tension in the elderly woman's body was palpable. Was she expecting Jake to hurt her?

'I'm not probing,' Jake said softly. 'I'm just touching.' He rested her hand in his left hand, and touched her damaged wrist with his right, running his forefinger gently up and down her arm, along her fingers, not pressing, smooth as silk.

'Stop me the minute I make you feel uncomfortable or I hurt you,' he told her. 'Stop me the moment I make anything worse.'

She didn't stop him. He ran his fingers over the back of her palm, over and over, and then cupped her hand and felt that, too. Around her Tori felt the tension ease. Everyone, it seemed, had been holding their breaths. Even Mrs. Matheson, who'd been clearing coffee cups, had paused, riveted.

'Press my hand,' Jake was saying. 'Here. One finger at a time. Can you clench? No? Don't try, then. What does that feel like?'

'Like my hand doesn't belong to me,' Glenda whispered. 'Like it's not there—only it is. I can feel it but not like I want to feel it. Sometimes it hurts so much I just want to chop it off. It's not mine any more. It's not real.'

'It is real.'

'I'm being stupid,' Glenda said, as finally Jake rested her hand in his again and let it lie.

'No.' It was such a flat response that Glenda stared. 'You're not being stupid. How long have you been putting up with pain like this?'

'A while.'

'Months,' Doreen said dully. 'And it's getting worse.'

'But at the beginning it did seem to get better?'

'Yes,' Glenda whispered. 'That's why it's stupid. It got better and all the scans are good and the doctors say I'm cured. Only then the pain started…'

'I've seen this before,' Jake said. He was still holding her hand in his, so gently he couldn't possibly be hurting.

'I'm thinking this is something called complex regional pain syndrome,' he said, and it was as if he was alone with Glenda—everyone else had disappeared. 'Everything fits. You've had major trauma. So many of the bones and blood vessels and nerves were damaged that often a physical recovery masks more complex nerve problems. The symptoms often occur months after the injury itself. Your hand feels cold and there are areas of sensory blunting. It feels strange and stiff, like it doesn't quite belong to you. And then there's the pain. You protect it to stop it hurting, and the more you protect it, the worse it gets. Your fingers are already starting to curl. It's hard to make them move.'

'I don't want to move them,' Glenda whispered. 'But it's only my hand. I was so lucky… I'm better.'

'You're not better. You have nerve damage that needs to be addressed,' Jake said sternly, and Glenda blinked and looked at him with something akin to hope.

'The doctors say there's nothing they can do.'

'That might be because you've been talking to surgeons,' Jake said. 'And no, there's nothing more surgeons can do. Now it's time to move to another specialty.'

'Like you?'

'Someone like me. I can't prescribe in this country—I'm not registered. But I'm happy to write a note for you to take to your family doctor, asking that you be sent to a pain specialist.'

'More morphine?'

'Morphine's not great for this type of pain,' Jake said. 'What you need is a drug specifically targeting nerve pain, and there are good ones. My guess is that we can give you immediate relief the moment we get you a nerve-specific drug. If you agree, first thing tomorrow we can find out who knows who in this valley and get you on something that will help.'

'I know people,' Tori offered, and Jake sent her a smile that made her feel even more dazed.

'There you go, then. First cab off the rank is our local vet. They say there are six levels of connection between you and anyone else in the world. I'm thinking Tori will do it in two.' And then, as Glenda looked at him in disbelief, he touched her cheek, a huge gesture, Tori thought, for someone who seemed to hold himself so aloof.

'It's okay,' he told her. 'The nerve-specific pain relievers are easy on the tummy, and it's not like you'll need them forever. You also need a hand therapist, and you need her urgently as well, if that hand isn't to turn into a claw. You think you might be able to find us one of those, Tori?'

'Dad's old vet nurse has a daughter who's a hand therapist,' Tori said, absurdly pleased. 'She works in the same clinic as the doctor I use.'

'There you are, then,' Jake said. 'But first…let's pack that hand in heat before you go to bed. We'll pack it in hot-water bottles, or heat packs if Rob's got them. We'll give you some of that morphine—yes, it has side effects, but I'm thinking this is the last time you'll take it—and then you'll sleep. That's an order.'

And he said it so sternly that, to Tori's astonishment, Glenda giggled.

'Yes, Doctor,' she said.

'That's what I like,' he said. 'An obedient patient.'

'Thank you,' Doreen breathed, and Tori looked from Jake to Glenda and then back to Jake and she thought, I am in such trouble.

Do not trust?

How could she not?

She didn't have a choice. Concentrate on work, she thought suddenly, fiercely. Jake was being kind because he was a doctor. Maybe she should think of a way she could be useful, too.

'Rob, tomorrow you and I need to talk about your pet policy,' she ventured, as Glenda glowed at her and then glowed back at Jake. She looked as if she might be as smitten as Tori was feeling. 'If you're giving fire victims time out, what they most need is the people and pets they love. Are you allergic to cats, Jake?'

'No, but…'

'But what?'

'But nothing,' he told her and shrugged and smiled. 'There don't seem to be many buts right now.'

Where was the aloof man she'd met at five-minute dating? He was unbending by the minute.

'You organise it,' he said. 'Tell Rob what he needs to do and he'll do it. What you're capable of…are you sure you're just a vet?'

'I'm just a vet,' she said, a trifle unsteadily, but Jake's smile was making her feel as if she didn't know what she was any more.

Do not trust.

'If you'll excuse me,' she said unsteadily, 'I'm really very tired and Rusty will be waiting. Goodnight, all.'

And because the night really was getting blurry—because she didn't understand how the expression on Jake's face was making her feel—she rose and fled, just as fast as her dignity allowed her.

CHAPTER FIVE

EXHAUSTION took care of the first part of the night. It almost always did. But despite the wonderful meal, the fabulous bed and the feeling of being nurtured, the demons were never far away. Tori woke as she'd done for the past six months, at three in the morning, to stare wide-eyed into the dark. Remembering a darkness she'd never forget.

Rusty had gone to sleep on her bed. Now, however, he was where he always was at this time of the morning, with his nose hard against the door, waiting for someone to come home.

'It's time we both stopped waiting for them,' she told him, but he whimpered and pawed the door and she rose to let him out, to show him that no one was on the other side of the door.

Rusty had been one of a pack. Maybe she should get a new pup, she thought. Maybe that'd help. Somewhere, sometime, she'd read that a measure of a life well lived was how many good dogs could be fitted in. As a vet and dog lover since childhood, she accepted that for a fundamental truth. But still… To take that last step and move on…

She wasn't ready and she wasn't sure Rusty was either.

She walked out onto the verandah and gazed up at the mountains looming above. The moon was vast and full, turning the night into a sepia version of daylight, with the blackened landscape softened, disguised.

Rusty nosed her ankle and whimpered.

'We shouldn't be off the ridge,' she whispered, stooping to hug him. 'It feels wrong.'

It wasn't wrong. She had to start her new life. Tomorrow?

But maybe she'd come down too quickly. Right now it felt as if she'd forgotten something very important.

'Maybe we need to say goodbye,' she whispered. 'Come on, Rusty, we can do this. Do this and move on.'

She slipped back into her room and tugged on jeans and windcheater, then headed out again, her little dog at her heels. She didn't go out through the house, though. She didn't want to wake the household, so she slipped out onto the verandah, down through the rose garden, around the corner of the house to the car park—and she barrelled straight into Jake coming in the opposite direction.

For a moment all her breath was pushed out of her. Shock left her speechless. Jake had caught her, steadied her by her shoulders, looked quizzically down at her. Then, as Rusty whimpered, he squatted and patted the little dog under the ear.

'Hey, it's okay,' he told him. 'I'm a friend.'

Rusty nuzzled his hand and moved closer to Jake's ankle. Which was surprising all by itself, Tori thought, feeling breathless. Rusty hadn't responded to anyone since his master's death.

'Are you running away?' Jake asked mildly, looking up at her in polite enquiry. 'Aren't you supposed to have a pole with a bandana slung over your shoulder? I don't think running away's proper without them.'

'We're not going far,' she managed, struggling to make her voice work. 'Why are you up?'

'I couldn't sleep,' he said simply. 'I had a whole lot of my preconceptions stood on their head at dinner. It's taking a bit of getting my head around.'

'Like, your father loved you?'

'There's a way to go before I'll believe that,' he said, and his smile faded. 'Words are easy. But you… You're going where?'

'Up to the ridge.'

'You forgot something?' He'd straightened. His gaze held hers, serious, compassionate.

'I… Yes.'

'Do you want company?'

'I don't…' She faltered. Say no, her head screamed. But there was something about this night. There was something about this man.

'We left too fast,' she whispered. 'Tomorrow Rusty and I will move on—we need to. We'll start a new life. But for six months we've simply been putting one foot in front of another, over and over, and in Rusty's case we've even lost a foot doing it. I thought… Tonight I wanted to just say…'

She faltered but his gaze didn't waver. He took her hands. 'Of course you do,' he said softly. 'Can I drive you?'

'I don't—'

'If you don't want company, then I'll wait here for you to come back,' he said. 'If you need to be alone, then I understand—of course I do. I'll sit here and wait, and see if I can get rid of my own demons, and if you don't come back by dawn, then I'll come up to the ridge and demand the ghosts give you back. You belong in the real world, Tori. Tonight the real world will look out for you. I'll look out for you.'

And she knew that he would. Trust? There was that word again, raising its ugly head, but the night was still and beautiful and Jake was watching her with a look that was non-judgemental, nonpossessive or needy. It was simply…caring?

The sensation was insidious in its sweetness and there was no way in the wide world she could resist.

'Then yes, please,' she whispered, stupid or not. 'I'd love it if you would come with me.

* * *

So they headed up to the ridge, with Jake driving and Rusty cradled on Tori's knee. Only instead of glancing out the window all the time, as Rusty always did, the little dog kept glancing across at Jake.

As did Tori. She didn't understand what she was feeling. She mistrusted the instinct that had her accepting his company, but for now Jake's presence was warm and solid and real, and strangely it made what she wanted to do feel even more right.

They drove past Jake's darkened farmhouse, the hub of so much activity over the past six months, and that felt strange. Then they turned into the drive of what once had been her home and that felt worse.

Even the night couldn't disguise the destruction. Blackened fence posts, massive trees, felled and not yet cleared, a gaping void in the blackened bushland where the house had once been.

A chimney rising out of the ashes like a lone sentinel, a monument to what had happened.

'I can't begin to imagine what it must have been like,' Jake murmured, and Tori shook her head, tears not far away. What was it with this man? She hadn't cried for six months. How could she cry now?

'I was in the valley,' she whispered. 'I couldn't get back. The whole mountain was on fire. I was going out of my mind. Everyone with people we love up here was going out of their minds. It took three days before we could get back. Three days...'

He didn't respond, just looked steadily out at the ruins, and she knew by his silence that he could see how it must have been.

She climbed out of the car, and he didn't follow as she made her way carefully over the ruins. Jake knew instinctively that she didn't want him to follow. Rusty came with her, limping by her side, but he had the right. This had been home for both of them.

Home.

If she could turn back time...

If only she hadn't trusted.

She picked her way across the rubble to the chimney stack. The fireplace was almost intact. A few bricks at the corner had fallen when a roof beam had dropped across the mantel— that's how Rusty had lost his leg.

She placed her fingers on the ledge above the fire cavity. There'd been a wooden mantel resting here, and on it an ancient clock that never kept time, pictures of her parents on their wedding day, pictures of Tori and Micki as kids, her graduation photo, Micki at some glamorous, want-to-be-model shoot.

This hearth had been the heart of their home, and in the end this small fireplace had succeeded in saving one little dog. One small thread to connect her past to her future.

At least Micki and her father had thought she was coming, she thought bleakly, letting herself think back as she so seldom allowed herself to do. That was the only thing that kept her sane—that last, frantic call from Micki.

'Tori, the fire's on this side of the ridge.'

'I've rung emergency services,' she'd said, as she pushed her van past the speed limit, heading into smoke so thick she knew she'd have trouble getting through. 'The fire trucks are on their way. I'm on my way. Stay cool.'

Stay cool. It had been their farewell line for ever, between two sisters and taken up as a joke by their father.

She'd said it then, with love; her sister had laughed, and she knew her father and Micki had died knowing she was moving heaven and earth to get to them.

And suddenly it was okay. Their ghosts were here now.

She could feel them, a soft and gentle presence. It was right to come tonight, she thought.

She'd loved her family more than life itself, and they were still with her, in this place. Rusty was by her side, pressing against her, a link to them. She knelt and fondled him.

'We can go on,' she whispered. 'I can't forgive Toby, but maybe…maybe I can forgive myself for trusting him. Dad and Micki trusted him, too. They wouldn't want me to beat myself up forever.'

Jake was waiting. Life was waiting. The night was still and warm, and the moon's gentle beams were almost a blessing.

It was time to go.

She straightened and turned. Jake was at the edge of the clearing, watching gravely from the shadows.

'I'm all right,' she said, managing a smile. 'I'm not about to wail or rend my garments.'

'I'm pleased to hear it.'

'Thank you for coming.'

'It was my honour,' he said gravely, and it was so much the right thing to say that she caught her breath. She picked her way back over the ruins but he met her halfway, catching her hands as she stumbled and helping her the last few steps.

'Okay?' he asked softly, and she managed a smile and a sniff, and if she left her hand in his, then who could blame her?

'It was so lovely here,' she whispered. 'I can't tell you. My mum and dad, my sister, our friends, our dogs, chooks…'

'Chooks?'

'Hens. All sorts. My dad bred Rhode Island Reds. They spent their lives clucking around the orchard. Can I show you the orchard?'

She didn't wait for an answer, but led him around the pile of rubble to a stand of small trees behind the house site. The fruit trees stood out from the trees he'd been seeing over and over up here on the ridge, for they weren't burned. They were a mass of blossom in the moonlight, on a bed of deep, green grass.

'The orchard's deciduous,' she said simply. 'Not native. They were so green in the summer that they didn't burn. The grass under them was dry and it burned but the trees themselves didn't catch. So now we have cherry blossom, and apple blossom, and peach. Micki and I had a big log swing hanging on the peach. One day I'll hang that swing again.' Her voice faltered. 'I hope.'

'You'd want to live here again?'

'It's my community,' she said simply. 'My home. Rusty thinks so, too.'

But Rusty wasn't looking around him. He was pressed against Jake's leg. He was forming a new allegiance, Tori thought.

Confused, she pulled away a little, and walked further into the orchard. A low-hanging cherry branch brushed her hair and blossoms drifted around her. She put her fingers out and caught them, and suddenly she found herself smiling. Rusty had limped over to the base of the oldest tree—the peach. The grass here was thickest. He wriggled down, burrowing his nose in the long grass, and gave a sigh of pure contentment.

It felt good. More, it felt great. For the first time in six months she felt free. The ghosts of her family were all around her, a gentle, loving presence that would do nothing to hold her back.

And Jake was here. Suddenly it seemed right that he was.

'You're beautiful,' Jake said softly, wonderingly, and she smiled at him and shook the branch a little, letting loose another cascade.

'Beautiful's how I feel right now,' she said simply. 'Thank you.'

'There's nothing to thank me for.' He stepped closer and plucked blossom from her hair. 'You're facing your demons all by yourself.'

'No,' she said gravely. 'How can I? Don't you know that all by yourself is a really bad idea. I sense you're a loner, Jake Hunter, but loneliness isn't for now. Not for tonight.'

And then, because she didn't know why—the night, the warmth, the smell of blossom, the sight of Rusty wriggling contentedly in the grass that was once his favourite place, the feel of this man's hand brushing her cheek as he lifted blossoms away—for some a reason she would never understand, she stood on her tiptoes and she kissed him.

Loneliness isn't for now....

For Jake, too, this day had been huge. He'd come to this country to put his property on the market and depart, cutting the links to a father he held in dislike, even contempt.

But things had changed. His view of the past, taught to him by a bitter woman, had been challenged by an unbiased witness and had been found wanting.

There were emotions in his head that matched Tori's, and now Tori's tragedy was layered on top of his. He couldn't figure out what he was feeling.

But he didn't have to figure it out. Tori was doing it for him. Her mouth was on his, her body was pressed against him, and all he could feel was her sweetness, her gentleness, the beauty of this night.

He wanted her.

And as if she'd read his thoughts...

'I want you,' she whispered.

His hands tightened involuntarily on her waist and he was pulling her against him with a hold that was entirely proprietary, entirely sure of what he wanted. Tori.

Quite simply she was the most beautiful woman he'd ever

met. She was in battered jeans and trainers, an ancient wind-cheater; her curls were all over the place, her eyes were huge in her too pale face.

She was gorgeous and he wanted her.

This was some sort of magnetic attraction he'd never met before, some primitive link, some compulsion he didn't fully understand.

Who was he kidding? He did understand it. He wanted her, as simple as that. Something tonight had pulled him to her in a way he didn't understand, but he wasn't questioning it. It was the way her hands held his, the way she looked up at him in the moonlight, the way she tugged him closer, closer, so he could no longer see her face, so all he could do was feel the beating of her heart.

They both knew where this was going. They both knew how right this moment was. But…

'I don't have a condom on me,' he said, in a voice so hoarse he hardly recognised it. 'We can't—'

'I'm protected from pregnancy,' she managed, breathless. 'So…unless we're talking multiple partners, we're okay. Toby and I…we tested.'

'I'm safe,' he growled, but sense prevailed enough for him to haul away from her long enough to rake his fingers through his hair. Knowing he should put her away from him. Knowing he must. 'Tori, you don't know me. You shouldn't trust me. You shouldn't want to.'

'I know. It's crazy, stupid, risky, crazy…'

'You already said crazy.'

'That means it's double crazy.'

'So we stop? We go sensibly back to the lodge?' He said it trying to keep his voice flat, inflexionless, as though she ought to agree to the sensible option. He was giving her the sensible option.

But who wanted to be sensible? Not Tori.

Sensible was for tomorrow.

She took a deep breath, her eyes not leaving his. She tugged her ancient windcheater up and over her head and she tossed it aside.

Her figure was perfect—and more.

Her bra was beautiful, made of exquisite lace, so white it was almost luminous in the moonlight. Her breasts were framed by the sweetly curving lace; they were soft mounds of perfection and they took his breath away. All of her took his breath away.

She'd kicked off her shoes. Now she pushed the zip and stepped out of her jeans as if it was the most natural movement in the world.

Her panties matched her bra.

He'd forgotten how to breathe.

'Not all the welfare bins held hand-me-downs,' she said, totally unselfconscious, grinning at the look on his face. 'A gorgeous Swiss lingerie company sent a care box. You like?'

Did he like? He was speechless. She was standing barefoot on the grass under the blossom tree, smiling up at him, all imp, in the most beautiful lingerie he'd ever seen. In the most beautiful body he'd ever seen. The contrast to the woman he'd met—how many hours ago?—was stunning.

'You're beautiful,' he said, and it was totally inadequate.

'My undies are beautiful,' she corrected him, and he tilted her chin and gazed straight into her eyes and he shook his head.

'*You're beautiful*,' he repeated, so strongly she had to believe him. 'But this… Are you sure? Tori, I want you tonight, I want you more than I've ever wanted anything in this lifetime. But I do need to go back to the States…'

'Your medicine's in the States,' she whispered, and she met his gaze directly, clear and true. Knowing, as he did, that this was far too soon for any decision to be made as to a future. 'This is no five-minute date, Jake, but neither is it any kind of commitment. This is seduction, need, call it what you will, but it's for tonight. It's your need and mine, for tonight and tonight only.

'I trust you,' she said steadily—and she knew she was right. For this night, trust had returned with a vengeance. She thought suddenly of Jake's father, of the elderly doctor she'd known and loved, and she knew that no matter how little he'd known him, Jake truly was his son.

Jake… A stranger, yet not.

Here, now, he was hers.

'I'm as sure as anything I've ever known,' she whispered. 'My body wants you. I want you.' And she fumbled with the catch to her bra.

But he was before her, unfastening the clasp, then cupping her breasts, caressing, holding, teasing her nipples, sending fire surging through her body, blocking out all else.

This was so right. This was…now.

Crazy but right. Stupid but wonderful.

Perfect for now.

Her body was on fire.

Not crazy. Not stupid.

Perfect.

He was touching each nipple in turn with his lips, reverent, wondering, and she arched back, hot with want. It felt so good, so wonderful, to be lifted out of the past six months, to feel the grey fading away like some forgotten nightmare.

Her body was surging to his touch, a bud unfurling in a blast of heat, coming to life in ways she'd never felt before.

Jake.

She should be embarrassed. She should at least be a little self-conscious.

She felt nothing but right. His gaze told her she was beautiful and for tonight she believed that message absolutely.

'I believe things are a little unequal,' she managed, and

somehow she unfastened his shirt, button by button, a slow, inexorable path of exploration, while he kissed her lips, her breasts, the nape of her neck, trailing kisses downwards while she tried to concentrate on undressing him. His shirt was gone, his belt, his chinos, and then, finally, he was kicking them aside and all his clothes had disappeared. Her skin met his as he tugged her close, closer, her body curved into his and fell onto the bed of soft, lush grass.

They gasped as one as the coolness of the grass met their bodies. They were clinging to each other for warmth, for heat, waiting for the loving to take over and for the cool of the night to disappear.

As it did. As it must.

She wanted him. She ached for him as he kissed her, deeply, searchingly, wonderfully, as his fingers explored every contour of her body, as her breasts moulded to him, as their heartbeats synchronised.

She wanted him, wanted him, wanted him....

Skin against skin, full-length, she had him all. *He was hers.*

She was riding his body, mounting him, holding him hard under her. She was aching, aching.

'Tori,' he whispered, and then he groaned and then there was no space for words at all. For finally, searingly, wondrously, he was a part of her. His rhythm was her rhythm, his body was her body—skin merging into skin, body merging into body, and the night was dissolving in a haze of heat and want and pure, wondrous delight.

She loved. For tonight, she even trusted. For tonight, this was her man.

CHAPTER SIX

SOMEWHERE towards dawn they made their way back to the lodge. Jake drove. Tori sort of…wafted. She felt beautiful. She felt cherished. More.

She felt as if her world had transformed—like the grey had shifted and the sun was shining through. It marked an end of the dreariness, she thought, and as Jake refused to let her walk but carried her from the car to the house—and that meant carrying Rusty as well because she wasn't letting him go—she felt as if she'd moved to another life.

The dawn was beginning to glimmer over the mountains. When the household woke, life would begin again.

Life on the other side…

'You're smiling like the cat that got the cream,' he murmured, as he climbed the verandah steps and her smile broadened.

'I believe I am. I believe I did.'

'Tori…'

'No.' She reached up and touched his lips. 'Not a word. Nothing. That was just…perfect. It woke me up. It was like life started again. I don't know if you can understand.…'

'All I understand is that you're beautiful. Can I carry you to my bedroom?'

'No,' she whispered. 'I don't want to wake up beside you.'

Something shuttered in his face—an expression she didn't like. Pain? No. It was a closing of something that had barely started to open.

'Jake, no,' she said, swiftly—she did *not* want to hurt this man but this was important. She was struggling to explain it, struggling to understand it herself, but somehow she had to find words for what she was feeling. 'What happened tonight was magic, time out of frame. I needed it so much—I needed you—and I'll be grateful for the rest of my life. But if I wake up beside you in the morning…'

'It is morning.'

'You know what I mean. If I wake up beside you, then I might hold and cling. I might even get needy. I don't want that. I don't want anything to mess with what we had tonight.'

I don't want to fall in love.

Where had that come from? No matter, it was there, hovering between them as if both had thought it. Who knew what Jake was thinking, but she felt it, knew it, and accepted that it was to be feared.

Love… After one night? She didn't think so.

She knew she had to move on. Somehow Jake seemed to have given her the strength to do just that, and she would not mess with it.

'I loved tonight,' she whispered. 'Tonight I loved you. But we both know our worlds don't fit together. Let's just accept tonight's magic and move on.'

'I'm not sure I can.' He was pushing open the door to her bedroom with his foot. 'To leave you here…'

'It's what I want.' Was it? No, part of her was screaming, but the rest of her was sensible and it had to be sensible for all of her.

'You're so…'

'And so are you.' And then she paused. They both paused. Tori's room was right at the end of the house. The room next to hers was Doreen's. From the other side of the wall came the muffled sound of terror. Whimpering, sobs of fear. Real pain.

They couldn't ignore it. Neither of them could. Tori slid down from Jake's arms and slipped Rusty onto the bed, but before she'd straightened Jake was heading out the door.

She reached him before he reached Doreen's door, tugging him back.

'Let me. She knows me.' She knocked. 'Doreen, it's Tori. Can I come in?'

'I… No. Oh, my dear, did I wake you?' It was a breathless gasp. 'I'm so sorry.'

For answer Tori opened the door a sliver. Jake was beside her, but she motioned him to stay where he was. She slipped in, but she left the door open, just a little, so Jake could hear.

'Doreen, what's wrong?' she asked, and then, as her eyes grew accustomed to the dim light and she made out the figure huddled among the vast nest of pillows, her heart wrenched. She was with her in a heartbeat, gathering the elderly woman to her, simply holding.

'Oh, my dear, don't tell Glenda,' Doreen gasped.

Jake stayed outside, silent as a panther. She couldn't hear him, but she knew he was there, waiting to see if he was needed.

'You mustn't tell Glenda,' Doreen gasped again. 'She's asleep at last. It's just angina. Nothing. It hurts and I wake up and you know how the night terrors take over.'

Of course she did. Night terrors must surely be reality for every person who'd been on the ridge that day, Tori thought. But as she held her, as she felt her thin frame shake, she thought this was more than nightmares. And maybe more than angina, too? Her hands were cold and sweaty and she could feel her tremors. She put her fingers on her neck, finding her carotid pulse. It was fast, erratic, frightening.

'Doreen, I'm not sure this is just angina,' she said, trying to keep her voice steady, not wanting to put fear into the equation as well. 'I think we should get this checked. Can I call an ambulance?'

'No!'

'At least let me call Jake.'

'No,' Doreen whispered, but she said it much less force-fully—and then she stopped breathing.

One minute she was sitting on the edge of her bed, half supported by Tori. The next she simply swayed backwards, falling onto her pillows, unconscious.

Tori's fingers had been on her neck, feeling her pulse. Her hand followed her down—and there was no longer a pulse.

Doreen had said not to call Jake. That was five seconds ago. This was now.

'Jake,' she yelled at the top of her lungs. 'Jake, I need you *now*.'

He was with her before she'd stopped yelling. She was still searching for a pulse, but with her other hand she was hauling Doreen's legs back onto the bed, shoving away the bedclothes that were half covering her.

'She said angina. I think now…cardiac arrest. No pulse.'

Jake was on the other side of the bed, like her, searching for a pulse, then hauling pillows away, lying her flat, checking her airway.

'Breathe for her,' Jake snapped, and took the neckline of Doreen's flannelette nightgown and ripped it to the waist. His big hands rested on Doreen's chest for a moment, steadied, then moved rhythmically into cardiac massage. 'Breathe,' he snapped at her again. 'Tip her head back, hold her nose and fill her lungs with your breath. Twice. Then I pump. Come on, Tori.…'

She needed no third bidding. She breathed while Jake took a short break from chest compressions. Fifteen pumps per minute, down, down, down, while Tori breathed and prayed and breathed and prayed and breathed and prayed.

They needed an ambulance, defibrillator, oxygen, adrenaline, but there was no time, no space, to call for help. If they didn't get Doreen back now, no amount of equipment or expertise would help her.

No more deaths. Please, no. Not Doreen.

Breathe and pray. Breathe and pray.

'Don't panic,' Jake said softly and he must have sensed rather than felt her surge of despair. 'Steady, Tori, slow and steady, don't stop breathing until you've seen her chest rise.' He wasn't altering his rhythm. Down, down, down, over and over, over and over.

How long now? Please, please…

'Early days,' Jake said. 'Two minutes, no longer. Big breaths, Tori, deeper, I'm going harder.'

He did, and she heard the unmistakable sound of a rib cracking. She winced but kept on breathing, kept on breathing. Another crack. And then…

A ragged, heaving gasp, so harsh it caught them both by surprise. Doreen's whole body shuddered. Tori drew back a little, hardly believing, but Doreen dragged in another breath and then another.

Life.

Jake was hauling her onto her side, clearing her mouth again, supporting her, making sure she didn't gag, choke, while Tori sat back on her heels and stared and felt sick to the stomach. And then suddenly…not sick.

She could hear Doreen breathe.

Itsy bitsy spider, climbed up the waterspout…

Where had that come from? It was weird little song, a child's tune from her past, and suddenly as she watched Jake work, as she waited to see that she was no longer needed, that she was free to go for help, the song was in her head. Her mother had taught it to her. She remembered sitting on her mother's bed singing it. And then after her mother's funeral, she remembered her father bringing home two puppies, one for her and one for Micki.

'I'm calling him Itsy,' she'd told her father, and Micki had called her puppy Bitsy. She thought suddenly, crazily and totally inappropriately, if Doreen lived, then she wanted another dog and she wanted to call him Itsy. It was part of her prayer.

Doreen's breathing was steadying. Tori was grinning like a fool, and Jake's smile was almost as wide as hers.

But he wasn't relaxing yet. His smile was there but it was intent, and his attention was totally fixed on Doreen. He was moving on, she thought, totally concentrated on medical need. She, however, could back away a little. With Doreen's breathing settling they could risk Tori leaving for a moment.

'Call the ambulance,' Jake said. 'You have mobile cardiac units here?'

'MICAs, yes. Mobile intensive-care ambulances.'

'That's what I want and I want them here yesterday. Then wake Rob. I want the first-aid kit he keeps. We have oxygen. Move, Tori.

She moved. She might be a vet and not a doctor but she didn't have to be a doctor to know the situation was still grave. Something had stopped the flow of blood to Doreen's heart, and that something was still not resolved.

'See if Rob has dissolvable aspirin,' Jake snapped, and then as Doreen's eyes widened, focused, his tone changed. He sat down on the bed beside her and he took her hand in his.

'Hey, Doreen, you've given us all one hell of a fright,' he told her, as Tori headed for the door. 'You passed out on us. I'm supposed to be an anaesthetist, not a cardiologist. And I'm not supposed to practise medicine in Australia. Are you trying to get me into trouble?'

He was wonderful, Tori thought dreamily. She fled.

* * *

When the ambulance arrived it came complete with its own paramedical team. They moved swiftly and efficiently, and Tori and the now wide-awake Rob were no longer needed. And Doreen still wouldn't let them wake Glenda.

'She hasn't slept for weeks,' she whispered. 'I checked on her before I went to bed and she was sleeping like a baby. Please don't wake her. I don't need anyone to go with me.'

'I'll go with you,' Tori said.

'I don't need anyone.'

'Of course you do.' Tori smiled down at her, the events of the night making her feel spacey and happy and floaty. Nothing would happen now. Jake had saved Doreen. And somehow…somehow it felt as if Jake had saved *her*. The leaden weight that had hung around her heart for six long months had lifted.

She glanced down as something brushed against her leg and it was Rusty, but he wasn't brushing against her. He was simply positioning himself so he could press more closely against Jake.

You and me both, she thought mistily, and then Doreen's hand reached out and took Jake's and she thought, You and me, three?

'Could you come with me?' Doreen whispered to Jake, and the force she'd used to forbid them to wake Glenda was gone. She sounded frail again, and frightened. 'You're Old Doc's son.'

'I'm—'

'That's a really good idea,' Rob said, sounding relieved. 'It'd be great if she had a doctor go with her.' In case she arrests again. It was unspoken but definitely implied.

And for reasons of her own, Doreen agreed. 'Old Doc's son,' Doreen whispered. 'Combadeen has its doctor back.' Her hold on Jake tightened. 'It's so good to have you home.'

* * *

Who could sleep after that? The ambulance left, with Doreen and Jake aboard. Despite Rob's protestations Tori sat on the verandah and watched the dawn. Rusty was watching the road again, but things had changed. Who he was watching for had changed.

'There's no use changing your allegiance in that direction,' she told him. 'But as a transitional tool he's very useful.'

The only problem was, Jake didn't seem like a transitional tool. He felt permanent.

But, of course, he wasn't.

When she'd run into him tonight he'd been shocked to the core, thrown out of kilter by what he'd heard about his father. He had a lot of thinking ahead of him.

She'd seen his face as he'd followed Doreen to the ambulance. There was no choice in what he had to do. He'd care for the old lady, he'd do his best, but he was thrown.

What had Doreen said? He'd come home.

He was a long way from home.

She was sitting outside Glenda's bedroom. The French windows were open, and when finally she heard her stir she went in to tell her what had happened. To her surprise Glenda seemed almost relieved.

'I knew something was wrong. I've been so worried, but all she'd do was worry about me. I had to pull her out of the fire. I was sure she'd collapsed and it wasn't from the smoke but everyone was so busy… They just treated the burns.' She sat up in bed and nursed her bad wrist and she looked almost happy. 'And Old Doc's son is with her. Jake. Jake's home. I'm sure she'll be fine.'

She had breakfast, refusing to be worried, her faith in Jake absolute. When Rob offered to take her to the hospital, to relieve Jake, to bring him home, she accepted with pleasure.

They left—and finally Tori went back to bed.

Jake's home?

It didn't make any sense at all, but it kept playing, and she slept with it in her head.

Jake's home.

It was midday before Jake drove Rob's car back to the lodge.

Doreen had been transferred to the large teaching hospital in the city—without Glenda accompanying her. Stubborn and Independent R Us, described the two sisters, Jake thought wryly. They worried about each other and not themselves. Thus, 'You stay here and get that hand seen to,' Doreen ordered Glenda as she was wheeled away to the waiting ambulance on her way to get a cardiac stent.

Rob offered to stay on with Glenda. He had things to do in town and was happy to wait, if Jake came back later in the afternoon to pick them both up. That should have left Jake free to return to the lodge, but the Combadeen hospital was short-staffed, and once she'd heard the story of Glenda's hand, once Glenda told her what Jake did for a living, the local doctor grabbed him and held.

'If you're an anaesthetist I'd like some solid advice,' she said, so firmly he had nowhere to go. 'I can't get Glenda into see a specialist before the end of the month, yet I can't have her in this level of pain until then. If she'd told me…'

It seemed she hadn't. Discharged from hospital, Glenda had made perfunctory follow-up visits to the city outpatients and then had simply ceased complaining.

'Neuropathic pain's horrible,' Dr. Susie Fulton said gently to Glenda, still fixing Jake with a gimlet eye. He wasn't escaping on her watch. 'But anaesthetists are better at diagnosing it than family doctors. So can you bear Dr. Hunter examining you fully, so he can tell us what he thinks is going on? That way I can care for you until we get you some specialist help.'

'Jake *is* specialist help,' Glenda said stoutly. 'He's Dr. McDonald's son.'

'Charlie McDonald?' The plump little country doctor straightened and beamed. 'Charlie's son? Oh, my dear, have you come home?'

'No,' Jake said shortly. 'This is not my home.'

But as he examined Glenda with a lot more care than he'd done the night before, as he gave solid advice, and then finally as he drove back to the lodge, the phrase kept playing in his head.

Had he come home?

Of course he hadn't. This could never be home.

Why not?

It didn't make any kind of sense. This was the place his mother hated.

'The walls closed in on me in that place,' she'd told him. 'Everyone knew everyone else's business. You couldn't get away. Your father was everyone's best friend. Everyone thought he was their own property. Everyone thought I was their property. It's claustrophobic—people clutching you, needing you, you can't imagine.'

He could imagine. Doreen had clutched him, and as soon as Glenda arrived at the hospital she'd done her own clutching. Then the local doctor. Even Rob...

'Great that you were here,' he'd said. 'You know, if you were to consider staying, this valley needs doctors more than it needs rain.'

It was as though he was being hammered. Too much had happened too fast. And on top of the myriad emotions he was feeling towards a family he felt he no longer knew, he'd made love to a woman who'd twisted his heart.

Was it only two days ago that he'd met her?

Disturbed, and tired beyond bearing, he pulled the car over to the verge and closed his eyes. He desperately needed to sleep. A power nap would keep him going, and it'd also clear his mind. He'd used this technique often during his career, when things were closing in on him, seemingly too difficult. He'd simply stop, clear his mind of everything, sleep a little and, when things percolated back, the white noise would be gone and only the urgent issues would stay.

He lay back in the car seat, letting everything fade. Maybe he slept for a little. When he opened his eyes a flock of white cockatoos had landed in the paddock beside the car. They were screeching and wheeling like something in an Alfred Hitchcock movie.

And yes, things were clearer.

No matter the pressures mounting on him, he didn't belong here. No matter that it had been his father's home, it wasn't his home. The screeching of these unfamiliar birds cemented it.

But Tori…

Tori was different. The thought of her was front and centre in his mind, still right where she'd been when he'd gone to sleep. She was one special woman.

The white noise was the claustrophobia of this environment, of the needs of this valley. That had to be removed. It had nothing to do with him. Tori was separate.

Maybe they couldn't be separated.

Well, if not… He had no place here. His life, his work, his future were in Manhattan. The past two days had changed nothing.

Except he might have fallen very hard for a woman called Tori.

Tori rang the hospital as soon as she woke. 'Things are fine,' Susie told her. 'Doreen's already in Melbourne North Western. She's seen a cardiologist and they're putting a stent in later this afternoon. It seems a relatively straightforward block and amazingly there looks to be little long-term damage. He thinks she'll be fine. Glenda's still here. Jake told me your suggestion about the hand therapist, and she's with her now. Jake's lovely, by the way. Glenda says he was your five-minute date. How about that?'

She blushed. Nothing was secret in this valley.

'He's nothing to do with me.'

'No, dear, but if you could have him be something to do with you I'd very much appreciate it,' Susie said briskly. 'The valley needs someone like him so much, and his father's reputation has gone before him. People would trust him.'

'He lives in the States.'

'He has houses here,' Susie pointed out. 'So if you could think of any way to make him stay…'

'Suse…'

'Just saying,' Susie said and laughed. 'Is he home with you now?'

'No.'

'He should be soon, then. Rob's got a couple of things to do in town. The arrangement is that Jake'll bring back the car at five and pick up Rob and Glenda, so that gives you a whole lot of time all by yourselves. So see what you can do, my dear. I've been advertising for a partner for years. If you can do it with one five-minute date I'll be very pleased indeed.'

She chuckled and disconnected. Tori stared at her phone as if it was poison.

The valley gossips had been at it already.

No one knew about last night. All they knew was that she'd walked out of a five-minute date, and she was sharing a house with Jake. Yet already… Already…

She felt her cheeks flush. Jake would hate it. She hated it.

She would not have last night sullied by gossip.

So move on, she told herself. Move on fast. Jake was on his way home. She needed to be out of here.

Make another phone call.

'Yes, of course,' she was told by a women whose sympathy

was matched with the efficiency of six months' post-bushfire organisation. 'You've been almost the last one left living up on the ridge. There're three homes left in our relocatable village. You can take your pick.'

Feeling more and more panicked, Tori decided she could sort her gear later. She gathered Rusty and headed out the drive.

She turned out the stone entrance—and almost hit Jake coming in.

She stopped. It was only courteous. She had to say goodbye.

She'd made love to this man. What had she been thinking?

She knew exactly what she'd been thinking.

He climbed out of the car and she was caught again by how good he looked. Yes, his pants were creased and when she looked closely there were a couple of grass stains on his shirt. He needed a shave. His hair needed a brush.

He looked incredibly hot.

He climbed out and smiled at her and hot didn't begin to describe it. He made her heart turn over.

'Where are you going?' he asked, peering in her passenger-side window and Rusty practically turned himself inside out in order to reach him. Tori pressed the window button, the window slid down and Rusty was in Jake's arms in a flash. Jake submitted to being licked, and even laughed as the little dog squirmed his ecstasy in finding his friend.

His friend. Her friend. This man was seriously, seriously sexy.

'I'm going to see my new home,' she said, frantically attempting to firm something inside her that felt very much in need of firming.

'Can I come with you?'

Could he come? Um, no. Um, not wise.

But Rusty was licking his nose again, he was laughing and what was her head doing, saying no? Of course he could come. She could no sooner deny this man than fly.

'Of course,' she said, and he opened the door and climbed in. Uh-oh. Where was her escape plan now?

'You don't have anything else to do?' she asked, half hopeful.

'I need to be back at the hospital at five to collect Rob and Glenda. That's four hours.'

'You don't need to sleep?'

'I've slept.'

'You've slept?'

'For at least an hour. Any more is for wusses,'

'Right,' she said, thoroughly disconcerted, and restarted the engine and headed down the valley to her new home. With her man beside her.

Her man who wasn't her man. A Manhattan doctor.

Jake.

The relocatables were set up as a village. From a distance they looked like rows of shoeboxes lined up side by side.

Even from the road Tori could see there was no use checking out the three she'd been offered and choosing between them. They'd be exactly the same.

'What is this place?' Jake demanded, staring around in dismay.

'Home,' Tori said resolutely, heading for Shoebox 86. The key was in the door. She pushed it open and bit back a gasp of dismay.

Home?

Not.

She'd need to make it home fast, she thought, or the resolution she'd decided on would fail her. Somehow what had happened last night had seemed the catalyst for moving on, but now… Staying near Jake any longer seemed dangerous. This was the sensible option.

But this was *beige*. And Jake was still here.

So… She'd use him again, she thought. She'd use his energy.

'We need to shop,' she said briskly, but Jake wasn't listening.

'You can't stay here. It's like a budget motel.'

'It's better than a budget motel,' she snapped. 'It's new and it's comfortable and it's mine.'

'So what will you do here?'

'I've been offered a job in a pet clinic on the outskirts of the city.'

'Was that what you were doing on the ridge?'

'My father and I ran a horse clinic,' she said, 'with a small-animal practice on the side. There were scores of horse studs on the mountain. There's not a lot of horses up there now, though, and there won't be for years, so it's pets only.' A furrow appeared between her eyes and she shrugged. 'No matter. Last night showed me I can move on and I will.'

She was looking around, taking careful assessment. 'But you're right, I can't live here like it is now,' she said. 'I need to go shopping.' She glanced at her watch, hesitating. 'I should have come alone, but we have time before you've promised to pick up Glenda. If I wait until after then I won't have stuff today, and I need this place to be cheerful tonight.'

'You're not staying here tonight?'

'I am,' she said, flatly and definitely, and then she smiled, taking the sting from her words. 'Today's the first day of the rest of my life. Do you want to come shopping?'

Did he?

'There's—'

'Time,' she said, refusing to be deflected by his dismay. 'There's a great Asian trading centre a couple of miles from here. I reckon I could get all I need there and more.'

He stared at her, stunned. The difference between the Tori of now and the Tori of yesterday was, quite simply, extraordinary. What had happened between them last night had shaken his world, but for Tori it seemed to have marked a turnaround, transforming her from grief-stricken victim to woman about to embark on her new life.

'We should have brought the two cars,' she said, but cheerfully, as if she wasn't very sorry. 'You're welcome to stay here and wait. Or are you happy to watch me shop?'

She smiled and there was determination behind the smile. She might be transformed, he thought, but the grief was still with her. She was moving forwards, with shadows.

And the least he could do was come along for the ride.

'Shopping's my favourite thing,' he lied.

'Really?'

'No, but it's like hard work. I can watch it being done for hours.'

She chuckled, a lovely rich chuckle that had the power to transform this stark little apartment into something else. Tori's home.

Bleak as a great man's house without a fireplace in it....

The words came from...where? He hardly recalled the analogy, so why should they spring to mind now, dredged from literature or a play he'd once seen?

But he knew why they'd come. A house without Tori in it seemed the same. Unthinkable. She had the power to light from within, and that's just what she was doing as she grabbed her bag and jingled her car keys.

'Rusty's due for a nap. I bought him a doggy chew so he'll be happy enough staying here. You want to drive or will I?'

'I will,' he said faintly. 'I kind of like the challenge of driving on the left—and you should save your energy for shopping.'

CHAPTER SEVEN

So SHOP she did, while he stood back and watched in something akin to awe. She shopped with professional purpose.

Quilts, cushions, rugs, curtains, blankets, jugs, vases, wall hangings... There was little hesitation; she simply saw an item, beamed, picked it up, stuck it in her trolley, and when her trolley was full she used his arms instead.

'You're not leaving much time—or room—for milk and bread,' he managed, muffled under rugs, and she balanced another rug on top and steered him towards the door.

'I can get milk and bread after we've taken Rob and Glenda home.'

'You're definitely leaving the lodge tonight?' he asked, and she started unloading onto the register and tried to locate her purse among pillows.

'Of course,' she said absently. 'That's what this is about. I need to get my own place but I don't want to live with beige. It's only one step better than grey, and I'm not going there ever again.'

'It'd be good if you stayed at the lodge a bit longer,' he said diffidently, but she'd handed over her money, her hands were free and she could respond now with her full attention. She turned and faced him square on, frivolity gone.

'Good for whom?'

'You need to rest.'

'I wouldn't rest if I went back to the lodge. We both know that. Not with you around.'

The cashier, a bored teenager with lavender spiked hair, looked suddenly less bored.

'Well, maybe lack of rest has its advantages,' he ventured, fighting an adolescent urge to blush—but Tori shook her head.

'Any more than one night and I might get the wrong idea. No strings, Jake. You don't seriously want them, do you?'

'I…' How had they got here, so fast. 'No.' Was there any other possible response?

'There you go, then.' She was piling stuff back into his arms, tucking a pillow under his chin. 'Press down or we'll have pillows all over the car park. Can you manage?'

'Yes, of course.

'Then we're finished,' she said. 'Let's go.'

Conversation finished. She steered the talk onto inanities while they drove back to her new home and unloaded.

He'd never seen colour used to such effect. Within fifteen minutes the drab little relocatable had become home. Outside it was still a shoebox but inside it was the sort of shoebox a man might walk into and smile, because it looked exactly what his vision of Tori's home should be.

Even Rusty approved. He'd been staring dolefully at the door when they arrived, lying on the beige carpet. Now he was snuggled between two crimson and sky-blue cushions, with a purple throw-rug wrapped snugly around his injured lower half. He looked approving, Jake thought.

He approved as well.

'It'll take me a while to organise the curtains,' Tori said, glowering at the beige Venetian blinds. 'These might give us privacy but if anyone thinks I'm looking at them for more than a night they have another think coming. Now…' She glanced at her watch. 'Half an hour. I need flowers.'

'Flowers?'

'There's a flower farm half a mile from here. You want to come?'

Watch Tori buy flowers or stay here and wait? Of course he wanted to come.

Rusty decided to come this time, so he drove them both to the flower farm and she bought half a dozen daffodils and then two dozen tulips and then about a hundred gerberas in about three minutes, and then she decreed she was finished.

The word sounded too stark. *Finished.*

She had such courage, he thought, as they loaded the car and set off again. She was amazing. And more and more the thought of her staying in that sterile little relocatable—despite her additions—was almost unbearable.

But her face was set, determined, as though she'd made a decision and nothing was about to deflect her. She felt his glance and met his gaze and smiled, but he knew the smile was an effort.

He was leaving for New York. He couldn't help her. Even if he could, that'd mean getting involved—and he didn't do involved.

Did he?

Lots of things had to be thought through, he mused, fighting confusion. But in the meantime there should be something he could do. There must be some way he could help her.

And suddenly there was. They were driving past a farm gate, and a sign, roughly scrawled on a piece of tin propped against the mailbox, made him take his foot off the accelerator. Then, as the idea took hold, he braked, pulled the car onto the verge and stopped.

'Um, why are we stopping?' she demanded.

'We've forgotten something both you and Rusty need.' He was backing into the driveway and finally she saw the sign.

Golden Retriever Puppies. Ten Weeks Old.

'We don't—' she gasped.

'Yes, you do,' he said, and somehow he knew enough of this woman to realise his gut instinct was right. 'You had four dogs. You and Rusty have had six months by yourselves, and that's long enough. I have colleagues with dogs and I know how big a part of their lives they are. And I've met golden retrievers. They smile. You live in a place where pets are welcome—yes, I saw the sign—so why not?'

Then, as he saw her face, a mixture of distress and despair, he cut the engine, tilted her chin with his finger and said, 'Tori, you need something warm and alive and new, something not scarred by what's gone before. If Rusty hates it…if you hate it, then okay, but I do want you to think about it.'

She still looked distressed. He hesitated, unsure what to say, unsure what his feelings were. Last night this woman had moved him as no one had ever done. If he had longer… If it was possible, maybe she'd even penetrate the armour he'd built up around himself.

But for now, he couldn't leave her like this. Despite the colour and the flowers, he couldn't leave her in her strange little relocatable. Relocatable… Even the name seemed wrong.

This woman needed a home. Home was a strange concept for Jake, who'd always regarded home as where he could crash with least effort, but there was something about Tori that said home was much more.

'Last night changed things,' he said softly. 'They say men can take sex as it comes, and maybe they're right, most of the time, but they're not talking about what we had last night. It's bound me to you in some way I can't begin to figure. It made me feel like part of you is part of me. Whether that's dumb or not, that's the way you make me feel. Our lives don't connect. Not now. Not yet. But I can't walk away and leave you and Rusty without something of me.'

He glanced again at the sign. Maybe this was a cop-out, he thought, but for now it was all he could do. Anything else scared him stupid. 'So can I buy you and Rusty a puppy?' he asked again. 'From me to you.'

'So we get to hug a puppy in the middle of the night instead of you,' she whispered, in a voice that wasn't quite steady.

'Instead of nothing,' he said, and he heard bleakness but he couldn't help it. He hesitated, and then, because it seemed right, he kissed her, gently on the lips, and forced a smile. 'Though you can pretend it's me if you like. I hear golden retrievers make great tongue kissers.'

'Eww!'

He grinned. The distress on her face faded and the tension between them lessened a little. The kiss seemed to have made things better. It had made them seem…friends as well as lovers?

Friends *instead* of lovers.

Tori was smiling a little now, but she was chewing her bottom lip, looking at the sign, looking at him, looking at the sign again. Focusing on a puppy.

It was no small thing, he thought, to lose three beloved dogs and then to move forwards.

'Should I call him Jake?' she asked, and he blinked.

'Jake.'

'Big and warm and a bit shaggy.'

'Hey!'

'It fits.'

'I don't believe I'm shaggy.'

'You could be,' she said. 'If you loosened up a little. If you forgot to be a Manhattan millionaire.'

'I'm not!'

'Rob says you are.'

'Rob talks too much. I'm just—'

'A doctor doing his best,' she said, laughter fading. 'And your best has been wonderful. You saved Doreen's life last night. In a way, you've saved Glenda's. You're wonderful.'

The depth of sincerity in her voice was unmistakable. *You're wonderful.* He'd never been given such a compliment—by such a woman. And suddenly the light kiss he'd just given her was no longer enough. He desperately wanted to kiss her again—only this time deeply and long—but she was looking at the sign again, and there was a furrow between her eyes that told him her focus was no longer on him.

He had to back off.

'I guess…' she said slowly. 'I'm not working yet. It'd be a good time to get a pup. And it could really help Rusty.'

Okay, forget the kiss. Concentrate on what was important. 'It'd be a great time to get a pup, and I'd love to buy one for you.'

'I'd pay,' she said quickly.

'No,' he said, and he tugged her round to face him again. 'Manhattan millionaire, Tori. My gift.'

She smiled, a little bit wobbly but a smile for all that. 'If he's from a Manhattan millionaire, then he should have a diamond-studded collar.'

'He'd think it was girlie.'

'Then,' she said, her smile widening as she climbed out of the car, 'let's see if they have a girl. Jake might need to become Jackie. A golden retriever who doesn't sniff at diamonds. Jake or Jackie. Let's see what they have.'

She didn't choose a Jake. She chose a female and she chose a runt. Or Rusty chose a runt and Tori agreed.

He might have known. There were six pups as big as one another, as energetic as one another, as healthy as one another. There was one bigger than the rest, a male who obviously spent his life trying to round up his litter mates, growing more and more exasperated as his siblings didn't do what he wanted. And then there was a tiny female who tried gamely to join into the family romp and got knocked over every time. Rusty went straight to her, nose to tail, tail to nose, and they started, tentatively, to play.

'We nearly put her down,' the breeder told them, as Tori scooped up the pup in one hand and Rusty in another. 'My husband wanted to—she's such a runt—only she kept on fighting for her place at a teat and she has such courage that I couldn't bear to. But she's not right,' she confessed as Tori snuggled her under her chin. 'Her left ear is weird. It sort of sticks up when it's supposed to flop. And her tail's supposed to be long and feathery and I can tell already that it's not. The older she's getting the worse it's looking. If you want her, she's cheap.'

Neither of them was thinking of money. Jake watched Tori snuggle the little girl to her; he watched her with two dogs in her arms, and he felt great. This was going to work.

Then he got distracted. The biggest pup had been tearing round in circles. He had his litter mates rounded up, but then one of his sisters made a break for it. He darted after her, the others scattered and he had to start the whole process again. He practically beamed as he proceeded to bounce around the circle again.

He didn't know dogs. His mother had hated them, and now he spent his life at work. A dog was out of the question. But he watched Tori cuddle her two and he thought... He thought...

'Would you like two pups?' he asked her. 'I think the round-up guy's great.'

Tori's arms were full of wriggly dog. For a runt the little one had plenty of bounce, and Rusty was wriggling, too. They were practically turning inside out to reach each other.

'Two,' Tori gasped. 'Are you trying to drown me?' She sank onto the floor and was pounced on by a sea of pups. 'Oh, Jake, I shouldn't even think about one.'

She was half laughing, half crying. This was a huge thing for her, Jake thought, as he watched her hug armloads of pups. She'd lost three dogs in the most dreadful of circumstances, and she'd lost so much more. For her now to move on... To learn to love again...

'It feels like a betrayal,' she whispered but she hugged her runt closer.

'Grief has to let you go sometime,' Jake said softly. 'What did Auden say? Stop all the clocks? They did stop for you, Tori, but now they need to start again. Nothing is worth stopping the clocks for the rest of your life. And if that means loving again...'

'Says the man who doesn't do loving.'

'How did—'

'I can guess,' she whispered, smiling up at him through tears. 'I'm guessing your parents stuffed you so badly you've never got over it. So why don't you get a pup?'

'I work fourteen hours a day,' he said shortly. 'I can hardly leave one of these guys in a corner of the operating room while I work.'

'I guess you can't,' she said sadly, but then a tiny smile tugged at the corner of her mouth. 'As opposed to me. I'm a vet. I could take these guys to work. I could manage two dogs.'

'Not three?' He was still eyeing the round-up king, circler extraordinaire.

'Can you imagine that guy in my shoebox?' she demanded, following his gaze. 'My yard's the size of a pocket handkerchief. Even one's stupid. Maybe I shouldn't...'

Okay, he needed to focus. Forget the round-up king, he told himself, and he crouched among the puppies so he was right in front of her.

'It would be my pleasure to buy one of these pups for you,' he said. 'Please let me.'

Her gaze met his. Her eyes were glimmering with unshed tears, but she was trying to smile.

'A birthday gift?'

'When's your birthday?' he demanded, stunned.

'Today.'

'You're kidding!'

'Sort of,' she admitted. 'But that's what it feels like. My birthday. Like yesterday was one life and today's the beginning of another. Jake, last night…'

The breeder was watching, a big, broad woman in wellingtons and overalls, waiting for them to make a decision on the puppies. This was hardly the time to talk about last night. But…

'Last night was great,' he told her. 'And tonight…'

'Not tonight,' she said, fast. Her puppy wriggled to get down. She released him and the king immediately took it as a personal affront that his huddle of pups had been interfered with. He yapped and started circling again.

'Jake, last night was last night,' she said. 'It was the most wonderful gift. It's just made me feel alive again, like there's life still to come. So now… As you said, it's time to start the clocks again. So yes, Jake, I'd love you to buy me a birthday gift. My lopsided puppy. Itsy, I think, after a song my mother taught me.'

'Itsy bitsy spider?' he asked, bemused.

'That's the one.'

'My guy could be Bitsy.'

'Nice try,' she said and grinned and lifted up her puppy and held her, only this time it was almost as a shield. 'One pup. No more.'

There were so many conflicting emotions in his head he didn't know where to start. Business, he thought, and he grabbed his wallet and made a play of finding his credit card.

For suddenly he couldn't look at her. This woman with her arms full of pup. This woman whose life had been destroyed and was now starting again—while he went back to Manhattan. He need never see her again, he thought, and he felt suddenly, unutterably bleak.

Which was nonsense. He didn't do relationships, and he surely didn't do relationships with vets who lived on the far side of the world to him.

And he didn't do relationships with women he might just end up falling in love with.

But he looked at the play of emotions on her face as Itsy licked and licked. He looked at the errant curl that had escaped the knot she'd tied. Last night those curls had been down. He'd run his fingers through them. Soft as silk...

He wanted her.

'You want her or not?' the breeder demanded.

The dog. She was talking about the dog.

'I think we do,' he said, still watching Tori. 'Don't you, love?' She blinked. 'Love?'

'Figure of speech,' he said hastily. 'Don't you, um...'

'Tori,' she said and smiled, and it was as if she could read his thoughts. 'Dr. Nicholls.' Her smile held the memory of the night before. It was the smile of a woman who'd taken her man, who knew what he was....

Her man?

He belonged in New York, he thought, trying desperately to ground himself.

Remember relationships, he told himself. They never last. His mother had drilled it into him over and over until it was almost a mantra. 'Depend on yourself and only yourself. You fall in love and you start being stupid.'

Only his mother had lied. If she'd lied about his father, what else had she lied about?

But maybe in this she was right. Stupid would be taking Tori into his arms right now, and holding her, and…

And what? Carrying her back to New York? He surely couldn't see Tori in his sleek Manhattan apartment. She'd have to walk Itsy in Central Park.

He'd known her for, what, two days? So maybe in this at least his mother was right. You fall in love and you start being stupid.

He concentrated on payment. He felt Tori look at him for a long moment, and then she turned her attention back to Itsy.

Bitsy was chewing his shoelaces. He glanced down at the little dog and he thought Bitsy was the stupid side of him as well.

The breeder scooped him up and put him back into the pen. Bitsy looked out through the bars as if he'd just been put in solitary confinement.

'Will he sell?' He couldn't help asking.

'Oh, yeah,' the breeder said confidently. 'He's the best of the litter. I'm thinking, though, that I'll keep him myself for stud. Look at those bones…'

Bones? All he could see was eyes, looking out through the bars as if he'd personally betrayed him.

He glanced at Tori, who was also looking wistfully at Bitsy—while clutching Itsy and Rusty.

'I can't,' she whispered.

She couldn't. He could see that. They had to get out of here before they had the whole litter.

'Just Itsy,' he said.

'Just Itsy,' Tori whispered. 'Two is enough.'

Two dogs?

That was what she meant. She had her house now. She had her dogs. She'd start a new job, a new life…and he'd go back to New York.

What was wrong with that?

* * *

They made a fast visit to a pet shop to buy Itsy supplies. Then they headed back to the shoebox to drop off the flowers. They also did two medical consultations. It seemed that word had already spread that Dr. Nicholls had moved into Shoebox Mansions. They arrived back to find a border collie with a grass seed in its paw, and a corgi with flatulence, dogs and owners waiting patiently at her front door.

To Jake's surprise Tori took it in her stride—in fact, she even seemed pleased. While Rusty and Itsy explored their miniscule backyard Tori sat on the doorstep and turned into a vet again. While Jake and the owner held the big, docile collie still, she carefully tweezed out a cruel-looking hayseed. She cleaned the paw and disinfected it.

She then told the corgi's owner where to buy charcoal tablets, and to add a little yoghurt to her meals. Both owners went away happy.

'You'll be inundated,' Jake said, thinking of his mother; of the way she'd hated patients' demands.

'I like it,' she said simply. 'It makes me feel like I belong.'

He thought of his work; of the careful distance he kept. He worked long hours, but to have someone approach him out of context, a neighbour, someone in his gym…

This wasn't his world.

Tori wasn't his world, he thought. But how could he leave her?

Maybe he couldn't.

It was a bit after five before they arrived back at the hospital to pick up Rob and Glenda.

'We're a wee bit late,' Tori said, starting to apologise, but then Glenda spotted Itsy and no apologies were necessary.

Glenda was beaming. The new painkillers were obviously working. The tight lines of pain around her eyes had eased and, even though she was still cradling her arm, there was a huge sense of relief about her. Doreen had gone through the surgery with flying colours. The cardiologist had spoken to her and had been completely reassuring and Rob had promised to take her to see her tonight.

'And the hand therapist is wonderful,' she told them. 'He didn't do very much—he says I need really good pain control first and he's only going to work within the limits of what doesn't hurt—but he massaged really gently and I did tiny exercises, and already it's feeling better. He's given me a sheet of exercises to do at home, but I'm to come here every day because he says if we hadn't caught it now there might be long-term loss of function.'

There might already be a little, Jake thought, but he watched Glenda's shining eyes and thought a little loss of function would be nothing now that the pain was relieved.

'So we're both going to be okay,' Glenda said happily. 'But Dr. Fulton says we have to persuade you to stay here. She says anaesthetists make great pain specialists, and this valley needs a pain specialist so badly and if you're anything like your father you'd be wonderful. She says there're so many burns victims with long-term problems, long-term pain, that we all need you.'

And suddenly they were all looking at him. Glenda, Rob, Tori...even Rusty and Itsy.

'No,' he said, really fast, and Glenda's face fell. Tori's face didn't change, but he thought he saw the smallest quiver....

Don't go there.

'We need to get back to the lodge,' he said, still too fast, and Glenda took the hint and turned her attention back to Itsy.

'Is Itsy coming to stay?'

'I'm only coming back to get my car,' Tori told them. 'I've moved into my new house. Itsy and Rusty and I need to go home.'

Home. There was that word again.

'Oh, my dear, that's a shame,' Glenda said, throwing Jake a reproachful look—as if somehow he could have persuaded her to stay but had chosen not to. 'Oh, and Itsy would have made the lodge much more fun.'

'Where's your cat?' Tori asked her. 'Pickles?'

'In the cattery on James Street,' Glenda said. 'But—'

'Then let's go spring him and take him back with us.' Tori grinned happily at them all. 'Rob says the rule is no animals but I'm thinking he's the manager and Jake's the owner. Jake, your stepmother set the lodge up as an indulgence for the wealthy. That's gone out the window. What it needs now is to be a place people can come to recover. If I were you I'd think about pushing that aspect hard. Even when the fire's forgotten there'll always be people who need an interim place, between hospital and home. Pets are the first thing. Rob could make individual runs attached to the bedrooms. Guests can contain their own pet as much as they like, but still take it for runs or cuddle it in bed at night.' She hugged Itsy and Rusty. 'Like I do. It'll be great.'

And there it was again, that queer lurch he didn't know what to do with.

'Oh, if we could keep our cat…' Glenda said, while he tried to figure what exactly he was feeling.

'And you know what else? You could organise medical visits,' Tori said, and she was speaking directly to him now. 'Maybe you could set up treatment rooms so you could have visiting doctors, physiotherapists, hand therapists, counsellors, anyone you need.'

'You're talking staff,' Jake said, trying to focus on business when he just wanted to focus on Tori.

'You can afford it,' she said blithely and grinned. 'I chose a very cheap pup.'

'You did.' He was distracted, but his mind was on what she'd said. Manwillinbah Lodge as a health resort?

He looked at Glenda and he thought, It could work.

Maybe Rob would enjoy the challenge.

Maybe he'd enjoy the challenge, he thought fleetingly, but he stomped on that thought almost before it had a chance to reach the surface.

'Maybe,' he said, trying to sound dampening, but neither Tori nor Glenda would be dampened.

'It'll be lovely,' Glenda said, smiling and smiling. 'Doreen and I will come and stay all the time.'

'He hasn't said we can take Pickles yet,' Rob reminded her

'Are you allergic to cats?' Glenda asked, suddenly frowning. 'Like your stepmother?'

He knew nothing about his stepmother. 'I'm not allergic,' he said shortly.

'Do you like cats?'

'Yes, but—'

'Then there's no problem,' Rob said.

'You could buy a cat,' Tori told him, and they all looked at her. She coloured a little but held her ground. 'He… Jake said he couldn't buy a puppy because he works fourteen hours a day.'

'Do you, dear?' Glenda demanded. 'That's far too long.'

'Yes, but he could still have a cat,' Tori said patiently. 'Or better still, two cats. Cats are fiercely independent but they're still there when you get home at night.'

'You need someone,' Glenda said, and glanced at Tori, who was still colouring, and amended her statement. 'I mean…something.'

'I think I know someone with a litter of kittens,' Tori said.

'No!'

'No?' Tori said cautiously, and he thought he heard laughter behind her tentative query.

'If I want a cat I can get one in New York.'

'Yes, but will you?'

'No.'

'No?'

'I don't have room in my life for anything.'

'Or anyone?' Glenda said, forgetting to be innocent, and she was looking from Tori to Jake and back again.

'No,' Jake said, steadier this time, and firmer. 'And Mrs. Matheson will have dinner on. We need to get back.' And he swung himself into the driver's seat without another word.

She sat in the passenger seat holding her dogs, while Jake concentrated on driving. Rob and Glenda were chatting in the back seat. Jake was staring straight ahead and she thought there were things in this man's past that were hurting now.

She'd noticed the way he'd watched the crazy little male pup as he did his round-ups. He'd looked...hungry. She saw the same expression when he glanced at her. As if he was looking at something he wanted but couldn't have.

Fair enough, she thought. She felt a bit the same. Or, okay, she felt a lot the same.

They collected Pickles from the cattery. The ancient tabby purred with pleasure when Glenda collected him. He eyed the dogs with weary indifference through the bars of his cat cage, as if to say, If this is what I have to put up with to be free, then so be it.

But Tori's dogs weren't staying with Pickles at the lodge. She was taking them back to the relocatable tonight. Her new home.

She had an almost irresistible urge to stay at the lodge one more night, but she glanced across at Jake's set face and she thought, No, one more night would be one night too many.

Maybe last night had been one night too many—but then neither of them had planned it. It had just happened, a primeval need that had shocked them both.

Mrs. Matheson was on the verandah. She walked down

to meet them and added her voice to the chorus urging her to stay.

'No,' she said, sounding ungracious, suddenly close to tears. She thrust the dogs into Jake's arms and disappeared inside to fetch her possessions. When she came back out Glenda and Mrs. Matheson and Rob had gone. There was only Jake, leaning against her car. He was holding Itsy, and Rusty was at his feet.

He didn't look like a millionaire, she thought inconsequentially. He looked a bit rumpled, casual, nice.

Jake.

She had to go.

She thrust her stuff into the trunk and lifted Itsy from Jake's arms before she got teary. She put the dogs in the crate in the back seat, and she was right to leave.

She was ready to walk away.

'Jake…thank you,' she whispered, holding out her hand in an absurdly formal gesture of farewell—but suddenly she couldn't say anything more because he had her in his arms and he was kissing her, in a crazy way, in a way that said he wanted her, he needed her, she was his woman.

This had nothing to do with reality, she thought wildly, but she let herself be kissed. Of course she let herself be kissed.

And kissed and kissed.

This was still about last night. It was about the letting down of barriers—the beginning of her new life.

It had nothing to do with her wanting this man.

She couldn't want him. *She couldn't.*

But for just a moment, well, maybe for just several moments, she surrendered to him, and she felt her body light from within. She felt beautiful. She felt wanted. Jake was kissing her, holding her, her breasts were moulding to his chest, her feet were hardly touching the ground—and she felt all woman.

And when finally he let her go, when finally he put her

away from him and held her at arm's length, she felt as if her world was shifting.

She felt breathless and bruised...and like she couldn't bear to walk away.

And it seemed that neither could he. 'Come to Manhattan with me,' he said, and her world didn't just shift; it threatened to roll right over.

'Come to Manhattan?'

'Tori, this thing between us...'

'What...thing?'

'The thing that says I want you,' he said simply.

Simple? There was nothing simple about this. What was he asking? She stared up at him, dazed beyond belief.

'Tori, I don't understand this,' he said softly, tugging her close again, kissing her hair. 'I've never felt like this. I've never expected to feel like this. But now... I'm due to start work back in Manhattan next week and how can I leave? How can I walk away from you?'

'I guess...you don't have to leave,' she whispered, trying to make sense of what he was saying. 'You own two houses here.'

'This is my father's world, not my world,' he said, and suddenly he sounded more sure of his ground. He sounded forceful, determined, even a little angry that she could make such a suggestion. 'I'm an anaesthetist in a large teaching hospital. I'm good at what I do. I've worked hard to get there. But you and I...'

'You and I.' She said the words slowly. 'You and I? There's a "we"? Jake, you don't have room in your life for a puppy. Yet you ask me...'

'Plenty of doctors have wives.'

Wives. The word hung between them. It felt like a threat, Tori thought, suddenly bleak beyond description. *Plenty of doctors have wives.*

Was he asking her to marry him? What a thought. What a way to bring it up if he was.

'So…these doctor's wives…they don't need big yards?'

His brow snapped downwards. 'What the… That's not what I'm saying.'

'So what are you saying? You're asking me to marry you?'

'I don't know,' he said explosively. 'I hadn't even thought of marriage. But the way you make me feel… You just do something to me.'

'You're saying it's my fault?'

'I'm not talking about fault.'

'No,' she said bleakly. 'But you don't want this. To feel like this.'

'I can't pretend. I never intended to…'

'Of course you didn't, and I won't be proposed to against your better judgement,' she said, suddenly angry. 'To be slotted into your life in the few minutes you're home between work and sleep? In a place where there's no one I love? How can you ask that of me?'

'We could take Itsy and Rusty back with us. We could get a larger apartment.' He raked his hair and she thought, He really hasn't thought this through. He hadn't even known he was going to ask her to join him until the words were out of his mouth. Now he was trying to figure out how he could make it work. 'We could make arrangements,' he said.

'I don't want to make arrangements,' she snapped. Anger had arrived now, coming to her aid in a red hot mist. He thought he was attracted to her, so he'd take her home, like a puppy from a pet shop, without even doing the groundwork. *Plenty of doctors have wives.* What sort of statement was that?

'I'd take up space in your life, Jake Hunter, and you don't have space to give,' she told him, knowing she was right, even if it hurt like crazy to say it. 'My community is here. My work is here. My life is here. It's not sitting in some drab New York apartment waiting for you to get home at night.'

'It's not drab.'

'What colour is it?'

'Grey, but—'

'I rest my case.'

'Tori, this is stupid.'

'It is, isn't it,' she said, and suddenly, inexplicably, the anger died. For somehow she knew where he was coming from. He was as confused as she was, and as blown away by the unexpectedness of it. 'I know,' she said, much more mildly. 'You're feeling about me the way I'm feeling about you, like we have something special. But honestly, we don't. We had a…a frisson. Like a lightning bolt or something that shocked us and made us think we were special. Only you know what happens after lightning hits? You run in case it hits again. You don't want to be a part of my life, Jake, and I can't think I could possibly be part of yours. So let's just get over it.'

There was a long silence while anger dissipated. While sense prevailed.

'If that's what you want…' he said at last.

It's not what I want, she thought. But what did she want?

She wanted him to sweep her into his arms and carry her off into some magical happy ever after—only he didn't even have a yard for a dog. Where was the happy ever after in that?

'We need to say goodbye,' she said, struggling with her dignity, and Jake looked down into her eyes for a long, long moment and then finally he nodded.

'We do.'

Her anger was completely gone now. This was Jake, the man she'd loved last night. The man she could still love. The man she might even learn to trust. Anger was gone, but sadness took its place. Regret that a different time, a different place, could have worked.

'Goodbye,' he said softly, and she thought, I will not cry, I will not.

But then he smiled down at her and suddenly she didn't want to cry. She tilted her chin and met his gaze square on. This wasn't about loss. This wasn't about grief. It couldn't be.

Jake had been a watershed, a magical, romantic way to start her new life. He'd been her knight in shining armour, she thought mistily, and while the thought remained she stood on tiptoes and kissed him, lightly this time, and gently.

'My Lancelot.'

'Lancelot?' He sounded confused.

'You were my white knight, right when I needed you most.'

'A white knight,' he said, sounding revolted, and she grinned.

'Only for two days,' she said. 'While I played damsel in distress. Only now I'm not. So thank you, Jake. Off you go, then—back to New York, to your medicine. I wonder if there're more damsels in distress in Manhattan.'

'I suspect most women where I come from know how to rescue themselves.'

She didn't like that. It sounded as though she needed to get a bit of spine. She straightened and she pulled her hands away and she put as much spine in her voice as she could.'

'I'll remember you for ever,' she said, firmly and surely. 'I'm sure I could have rescued myself, but it was much more fun being rescued by you. Thank you very much, Dr. Hunter. I'm sorry I can't follow you to Manhattan. I'm sorry I couldn't buy Bitsy as well as Itsy, and I'm sorry you don't have a yard. Meanwhile we need to move on. We both have our careers to get back to.'

And somehow she smiled—and he mustn't know just how hard that smile was—and she climbed into the car and started the engine.

'Goodbye, Tori,' Jake said, but her car was already moving.

* * *

He felt sick. He stood in the car park of his father's lodge and watched until he could no longer see her car.

He'd let her go.

He had to. He'd asked her to come with him and she'd refused. What did she expect? That he stay here?

He thought back to the little scene back at Shoebox Mansions, to her impromptu clinic. People needing her. People expecting her to help at any time.

He compartmentalised his life. He'd go nuts if he accepted that kind of need.

But then... He turned and Glenda was on the verandah, watching him watch Tori leave. 'Oh, my dear,' she said and he thought, She understands.

How could she understand? She didn't know him.

She'd known his father.

Community.

No, he thought savagely. What had his mother said? It was insidious. It sucked you in.

His life was in Manhattan and he had no place here.

'Dinner's ready,' Glenda said but her message was much deeper.

'You go in,' he told her.

'We're waiting for you.'

It'd be a long wait, he thought. He had limits.

He was not his father's son.

'We're waiting,' Glenda said again, gently, and he gave up and walked inside with her.

He could do dinner. He just couldn't do the rest of his life.

CHAPTER EIGHT

SHE bought a sewing machine and hemmed curtains. Yes, this home was temporary. Yes, she'd eventually think about re-building up on the ridge or selling and finding something else permanent, but right now that decision still seemed too hard.

Sewing was therapeutic, trying to keep trailing drapes from Itsy. So was taking a complete break from injured wildlife.

So was letting herself think about Jake.

He was just a memory, she told herself, a gorgeous guy who'd helped her move on. He'd been her five-minute date who'd turned into her two-day stand.

But the thought of him still made her smile.

She should do something about getting a job, she thought as the days wore on. She shouldn't settle here and let herself dwell on Jake.

But she wasn't dwelling. Or not exactly. She was simply savouring what had happened. Why she felt different.

This morning she'd sewn for a whole hour. Enough. She wouldn't mind a small nap.

This must be the lessening of pressure, she thought as she and Itsy and Rusty headed for bed. It was another reason she wasn't accepting a job right now. She was too tired.

'We match,' she told they dogs. They got up and bounced

into frenetic activity for an hour or so; Itsy wore Rusty out, wore herself out and then, both exhausted, they slept.

Rusty loved it; he loved Itsy, and Tori loved watching them. But she was as exhausted as they were.

'We're like litter mates,' she told them, letting them sneak up to her end of the bed.

And she slept, dreaming of Jake.

He should have forgotten her by now, or at least he shouldn't be thinking of her as often as he was.

He needed more challenging cases, he decided. His patients were all too healthy. He worked steadily through a surgery list that he purposely left even longer than usual. He administered anaesthetic, he monitored his patients like a hawk—almost hoping for a challenge—and they stayed nicely stable and he didn't have to do anything and then his thoughts drifted to Tori.

He should ring her and find out how she was doing. Or not.

He'd rung Rob to find out how the new direction of the lodge was going. He'd spoken to Glenda, who told him how well Doreen was, and that she was back at the lodge already, that she was without pain and that she was getting better every day. Glenda herself was also better. She was starting to be able to grip with her hand. Her life was so much better without pain. Her cat was settling in. There were two more guests at the lodge now, one with a cat and one with two chihuahuas.

And when finally he got to talk to Rob and casually enquired about Tori, Rob said bluntly he hadn't seen her, and his blonde had given him the flick, so he was over women for the moment. Glenda was a bit more forthcoming, but not much.

'No, dear, we haven't seen her either. Wasn't she taking a job down in the valley? Doreen and I intend to find out where, so when Pickles needs his shots we can see her again. But Pickles's shots aren't due for another three months.'

Great. He was dependent for news on Pickles's shots. And he didn't have her phone number.

He wouldn't ring it even if he did, he decided. It'd mean...

It'd mean nothing. It was what friends and colleagues did. It'd make sense to ring and ask her how Itsy and Rusty were doing, whether she'd found a job, where her life was going.

He wanted to.

He didn't. He'd asked her to come to Manhattan with him. That request had changed things. Her anger had changed things.

He'd messed up their friendship, so he worked and he tried not to think about her.

He was currently on his fourth case for the day. The patient under his hands was an obese diabetic. All the signs said his triple bypass should be a nightmare, but every one of his vital signs was great. Every monitor showed normal.

The surgical team was chatting between themselves but they let him be. They knew Jake was normally silent. He had the reputation of being aloof.

That was the way he liked it—wasn't it?

Only...it meant there was time to think, and right now thinking was the one thing Jake didn't know how to handle.

She wasn't quite sure when she started thinking it, but when she did she couldn't get it out of her head.

It started with a vague sense of unease—a wondering about the sleepiness. Why was she so tired? And then she thought...

And then she tried not to think. Only she couldn't.

It was only that she was thinking about Jake too much, she told herself, but it had her trying to remember.

Her files had been burned along with everything else. The important dates were gone and her memory had holes in it.

Many of the people from the ridge were suffering like

this, she knew. Trauma had left gaps in their collective pasts. Post-traumatic stress disorder?

But giving a name to what was happening wasn't helping. Not when something else might be happening. Or might have happened.

She could phone Susie, she thought, only that'd give voice to her fears.

'Susie, when did I have my contraceptive implant put in? Am I overdue for renewal?'

She looked up the brand of her implant on the Web—cautiously—and found what she didn't want to read.

Effective pregnancy prevention for three years. After that, marked decreasing efficacy. Replacement must be undertaken within the three-year window.

Decreasing efficacy…

Surely she can't have been due to change. Surely she couldn't be that dumb.

Could she?

She wasn't ringing Susie, she decided. The problem with having a friend as her doctor was that her doctor was also her friend. She'd never be allowed to get away with a simple query. Like, when was…when *am* I due to change.

So wait.

She woke three weeks after Jake had left and nothing had happened—again. She showered and dressed and she felt too nauseous to face breakfast. She took Rusty and Itsy for a walk into town. She came home and she felt like a sleep again. Only first she'd just check out the package she'd brought from the local pharmacy.

She looked.

A thin blue line.

She stared at it for maybe ten minutes. It didn't change.

She tried the second packet.

Another blue line.

Shock held her motionless. Strangely, though, she wasn't devastated. She couldn't be. Even though she was stunned, there was a tiny part of her that admitted...joy? Dumb or what, but there it was.

Maybe subconsciously she'd been expecting it. The lethargy that had enveloped her for the past few weeks almost seemed to have prepared her.

She went out onto the front porch of her shoebox and stared at the distant hills.

She was pregnant.

She was twenty-nine. She had a great career—slightly stalled at the moment but ready to resume any time she wanted. She had heaps of insurance money.

She could have a baby.

She *was* having a baby.

Like Micki.

Her sister's face was suddenly before her, laughing, joyful. 'Tori, feel. He's kicking. My baby's kicking.'

Her hand went to her tummy and pressed. *My baby.*

And with the thought came a surge of joy so great it threatened to make her head explode.

'We're having a baby,' she told the dogs, trying the words out to see how they sounded.

After so much destruction... Life.

She was carrying Jake's baby.

'I'm going to have to tell him,' she told the dogs.

To not tell him was unthinkable.

Would he be angry? She deserved his anger. She'd promised him she was safe.

'It's early days, though.' She was talking out loud, thinking out loud. 'Something could happen.'

No. Both hands were on her tummy now, as if somehow she could protect it.

Nothing would happen to this baby.

'So tell him,' she whispered. 'Phone him tonight.'

She couldn't. She wasn't brave enough. He'd think she'd lied to him. He'd think...

'I have to explain,' she whispered, and then the phone rang.

'Doc Nicholls? We heard you were at a bit of a loose end. How do you feel about a flying trip to the States?'

CHAPTER NINE

THE last case had been complex and he'd welcomed it. Finally, here was medicine that held his full attention.

Jeff Holden was someone he'd worked with before. Jeff had needed surgery as a child and had recurring adhesions. Jake had recognised him as he'd come in.

Jeff had been allocated to one of his more junior anaesthetists, but almost to his surprise he'd found himself changing the list. Taking time to talk to him before he put him under.

'Do you watch baseball?'

'No.'

'Do you watch football, then?' he'd asked.

To his surprise Jeff did, and so did the nurse assisting, and instead of a tense few moments before theatre there'd been a heated discussion about Jeff's team—and while he worked he figured he ought to learn more about a sport he only took a fleeting interest in.

Now the operation was over—successfully, he thought, though with adhesions you could never be sure—and he thought maybe he could hang around until Jeff was properly awake. This surgeon was known as being curt. Jake had watched the operation. He knew the outcome and maybe he could answer questions.

Thanks to Tori he was changing, he decided, as he reversed

the anaesthetic and headed out into the recovery area. And as if the thought had conjured her…Tori was there.

For a moment he thought he was dreaming. He wasn't. She was in full surgical garb—she must, to be allowed into this area. She had green gown, green cap, green bootees.

Green eyes.

Tori.

She was chatting to a patient at the end of the recovery queue—a woman wide-awake and ready for an orderly to take her back to the ward.

Both of them were smiling.

She looked up and saw him and she stopped smiling. She said something to the woman in the bed, and she turned to face him.

'Hi,' she said. 'I believe you owe me three and a half minutes, Dr. Hunter. I'm here to collect.'

Shock held him immobile for all of three seconds. Now, though… He was across the room before he knew it, and he meant to take her hands, or he thought he meant to take her hands, but instead she was folded against him in a hold that felt good, felt right, felt wonderful. Her surgical cap was under his chin. He wanted to feel her curls, but they were in a hospital ward and she was gowned, almost a professional, and it seemed every one of his colleagues had suddenly found an excuse to be here.

How long had she been here? Had his colleagues known? Why hadn't someone told him?

'She wouldn't let us.' Brad, the oldest of the orderlies, answered his question before he asked. 'She came to reception a couple of hours ago looking for you. Marie gowned her and brought her in here.'

'I was just as happy in the waiting room,' Tori said, tugging away so she was at arm's length, and grinning happily up at him with that smile that had knocked him sideways a month ago and was still knocking him sideways now. 'But Marie asked me where I was from and we got talking and next thing I was in here. It's been lovely, watching everyone wake up, procedure over.'

'She's been talking to the Holloways,' Brad said, his gaze on Tori openly speculative. 'She's calmed them right down.'

The Holloways?

Jodi Holloway was seventeen with a diagnosis of kidney cancer. The parents had been close to hysterics since the diagnosis, but the surgery, performed by Central's most skilled urologist, had gone well.

'You know our Jim,' Brad said ruefully, still seeming to sense what he was thinking. 'If the great man says one more word than he must, it'll kill him. He told the Holloways there'd been a complete excision and the recurrence rate was on the outer edge of the normal curve, and then he went off to find his dinner. Only of course we had Jodie looking like death after anaesthesia and Mr. Holloway staring after Jim like he'd never heard a word and Mrs Holloway threatening to have hysterics. And here's your Tori, moving in like she's our own personal counsellor only better, saying, No, it's fantastic news, and drawing them a normal curve and explaining probability and saying, Wow, if Jodi's outside normal limits for recurrence, then there's only this tiny chance it'll come back, it's the best news. And by the time Jodie woke up she had both parents smiling. So if you don't keep her we will,' Brad said, grinning, and Jake realised everyone was grinning—practically the whole ward.

What was she doing here?

'Two and a half minutes now,' she said softly, for only them to hear. 'We need to talk.'

'I'm almost finished.'

'So you should be,' Brad said darkly. 'You started at six this morning and it's almost midnight. Take him home,' he told Tori. 'And he's not supposed to be on call tomorrow so you can keep him 'til Monday.'

'I won't keep him,' Tori said, sounding suddenly strained. 'I have a hotel,' she said to Jake. 'I don't want to intrude.'

'You're not intruding,' Jake said, feeling more and more as though his world had just lit up again. He didn't know why she was here but he was pleased to see her on all sorts of levels. 'Give me a minute to finish up here and we'll go find somewhere to eat.'

'At this hour?' she said doubtfully. 'Will anywhere be open?'

'Hey, this isn't Combadeen,' he said, grinning. 'I don't know why you've come, but welcome to Manhattan.'

She felt as if she was here under false pretences. He was acting as though he was really pleased to see her. She should just blurt it out now, she thought, but she had to wait until he'd spoken to the family of the guy he'd just been working on, and he'd checked his patient was fully awake and could take in what he was saying. So she watched and waited, calm on the outside. She was anything but calm on the inside.

But finally he was finished. He filled in his paperwork, they both got rid of their gowns and, at last, he was ushering her out through the hospital entrance.

He'd taken her arm as if he was genuinely pleased to see her—as though she was a favourite friend dropping in unexpectedly.

'You look great,' he said, and she smiled, but absently. She'd put all sorts of effort into her appearance but now she was too nervous to think about it. How to tell him?

'Why are you here?' he asked, and at least that was easy.

'After the wildfires we have lots of animals that can't go back to the wild. Zoos are offering them homes. I was asked if I'd come with a consignment of two koalas and four wombats.'

'To Manhattan?'

'Close enough.'

'Close enough to drop in for a visit,' he said and tugged her closer. 'So where are the dogs?'

'At the lodge. Rob's nursing a broken heart. He's a great puppy sitter. But, Jake...I needed to talk to you. I was trying to phone you. But then they asked me to come with the animals. There's something...'

They were in the crowded entrance to Emergency. People were bustling past them, intent, urgent. An ambulance was pulling up; people were spilling out. Life was happening all around them but Tori's life was centred right here, on this moment, and it could wait no longer.

'I'm pregnant,' she said, loud enough for a guy pushing a wheelchair towards the entrance to grin and say, 'Lovely news, dear. Come back in a few months and see how smooth I can push a gurney.'

Tori flushed from the toes up.

Jake stopped. They both stopped.

She knew what he'd say. She braced, waiting. No, she thought, wildly, she didn't know what he'd say; for there were two alternatives.

He could say, 'You told me you were safe.'

Or he could say, 'Whose is it?' Or, 'How do I know it's mine?'

She'd been trying to figure out answers to both, trying to force herself not to react. It was she who'd made the mistake. He was allowed to be angry.

But now... The silence was stretching out and she thought, Which, which...

'Hey, it's okay,' he said finally, strongly, catching her hands in his. 'Tori, don't look like that. We can cope with this. But you will have to move here.'

She blinked. This was so much what she hadn't expected. Simple acceptance.

You will have to move here.... She could ignore that, she thought. That was an aside. What mattered most was that he knew. She'd told him.

'I thought I was safe,' she started.

'So did I. I guess we were both wrong.'

'No, but I told you… I thought…'

'And I accepted your assurance because I wanted you,' he said, and his hands were firm and sure, imparting strength and reassurance. 'Tori, I know you well enough to accept you'd never lie about something so important. But hey, we're both medical. We both know the only true contraceptive is a brick wall. So where do we go from here?'

'I don't know,' she managed, shocked almost beyond speech. She pulled away a little and stared up at him, searching for anger. She saw shock, she thought, but no anger at all. Not even revulsion. Just a man taking in important news and trying to deal with it as best he could. A man concerned for her. 'Thank you,' she whispered, awed.

'For making you pregnant?' His mouth quirked at the corners and she thought, He's laughing. The concept of laughter right now was so ludicrous it was…ludicrous.

Maybe she wouldn't mind a bit more emotion, she thought. Was she reaching for the stars to want joy?

'I meant, thank you for not yelling,' she said, thinking it wasn't enough.

'Why would I yell?'

'Because I made a mistake. And…and for not asking me who the father is.'

There was a pause at that. 'I have too great a respect for self-preservation for that,' he said finally, grave again. 'I don't want to be kicked into the middle of next week.'

'I don't think I could kick you that far.'

'You'd be entitled to. Come to dinner. It's close.'

They didn't talk again until he ushered her into a late-night diner, where a guy called Louis greeted him by name and ushered them into an alcove he obviously used a lot.

'Burger and fries for me,' Jake said. 'Louis does the best. Would you like some, too?'

'No!'

'Dry toast?' Jake tried, sympathetically, and Tori screwed up her nose again and so did Louis, his eyes alight with interest.

'How about hot cakes with blueberries,' Louis said encouragingly. 'A nice short stack, guaranteed not to overwhelm a lady. And maybe a glass of wine?'

'Maybe hotcakes and tea,' Tori said gratefully, and Louis beamed and disappeared and Tori was left with Jake and his nice, sensible reaction.

She'd sweated over this moment for three weeks now. Tried to figure what to say. Now it had been said. She'd done what she'd come to do.

She didn't even need to stop and have hotcakes, she thought suddenly. She could go home. Only she wasn't going home. Not now. Not yet. She was sitting in a late-night diner with Jake, about to have hotcakes while he assimilated fatherhood into his life plan.

Sensibly.

Anger was rising again. Unreasonable? Maybe.

She wanted joy.

'How…' he ventured at last.

'I had a contraceptive implant.' She'd rehearsed this question. 'They last for three years. Only then my life fell apart and I forgot it was due for replacement. The night…the night we…'

'Made love,' he said gently, and she stared at her hands and nodded.

'Made love,' she repeated softly. 'It was love, wasn't it. Of a sort. All I could think that night was that I needed—I wanted—you, and I thought, Yes, I'm protected. Even afterwards I didn't worry. Only then, when I tried to figure it out, all my records were burned in the fire. As were Dr. Susie's, so the letters that were supposed to go out reminding people of routine stuff were never sent. So there you are. Comedy of errors. Resulting in one baby.'

'Our baby.'

'If you want a say…'

'You're not considering termination?'

'No!'

'Why?'

'Micki's baby died. There's been enough death. *I want this baby.*'

Louis arrived then, with their meals. The normally jovial host had sussed them out by now. He left, with only a sideways, speculative glance at Jake.

'So you came to Manhattan just to tell me,' Jake said.

'I don't want anything from you, if that's what you mean.' She concentrated on her hotcakes and left him to his thoughts.

There were a million sensations running through him right now—shock, disbelief that this could be happening, overwhelming responsibility…yeah, and a healthy dose of fear, too. But the one that suddenly hit the top was anger.

'You'll take my help,' he snapped, before he could control the anger behind his words. 'It's my call, too, Tori. You have my baby, then I'm in the equation, like it or not. You'll stay here.'

Her face stilled. She met his gaze steadily, but he thought he saw a flash of fear behind her eyes. What had she expected?

What was she expecting?

'No,' she said. 'You know where my home is, and it's not here.'

'Your home's burned. Your home could be anywhere.'

'In your dreams.'

'Eat your dinner, Tori,' he said, forcing his tone to gentle, and almost to his surprise she did. She nodded and addressed herself again to her hotcakes.

They seemed to agree with her. His appetite had deserted him but he ate his burger on automatic pilot while Tori made her way through Louis's truly excellent hotcakes. She didn't speak. She drank her tea, cradling her cup as though she needed the comfort of its warmth.

She'd done some serious shopping, he thought, watching her. She looked great, in tight-fitting jeans, high boots, a tiny white coat. Then he realised she wouldn't be able to wear those jeans for much longer.

She was carrying his child. She was alone and she was pregnant.

She had to stay—but he couldn't force her.

'I didn't mean to scare you,' he said, and she flashed him a look of mistrust.

'This is new territory for both of us,' she murmured. 'Scary territory.'

'People do it all the time.'

'Not me. Not us.' Then she shrugged. 'Look, this has been a big shock to throw at you. It's after midnight. You must be exhausted. I know I am. I'm staying tomorrow so if you want to talk about it again…'

'You're staying tomorrow?'

'I have a flight booked the day after. I thought I'd take two days after the delivery, one to tell you and one to let you come to terms with it and yell.'

She was only half joking. She'd expected anger?

There was anger, he thought, but the anger wasn't at her. It was at himself. He'd met her when she was at her most vulnerable. Why had he ever touched her?

'We can't undo it,' she said, evenly and steadily, seemingly forcing herself to be calm. 'I'm sorry to give you this respon-sibility you don't want. I'm not sorry for me, though, so don't you be sorry for me either. I'm a big girl and I can cope with this. In fact, I intend to love this baby. I suspect all Combadeen will love it.' She rose. 'Can I catch a cab back at the hospital?

'Where are you staying?'

She told him and he frowned. 'It's Saturday night. That whole district parties. There's no way you'll sleep.'

'It looked fine.'

'When did you arrive?'

'Four. I came to the hospital almost straightaway.'

'And I made you wait…' He was trying to get jumbled thoughts into order but it was like herding ants. All he could see was Tori's pale face, and all he could register was that this woman was carrying his child.

'Tell you what,' he said, noting her too-big eyes, the effort bravado was costing her, knowing half of her wanted to run. 'My apartment's got a great settee in the living room. There's more than enough sleeping space for two. I bought the place knowing I needed to sleep any time, so quiet's where it's at.'

'I don't want to stay with you.'

'You can trust me, Tori,' he said, gently but inexorably. 'Don't you?'

She stared at him for a long moment, a moment that stretched on into something far beyond trust for a night shared. It stretched into something that was important for their future. Shared parenting? And something more, he thought, but that was suddenly somewhere he didn't want to go. Not yet. Not ever?

'Let's get a cab,' he said, focusing on practicalities, be-cause practicalities were all he could bear to think about. 'I'll take you to your hotel. If I'm exaggerating—if you think you can sleep there—then I'll leave you and we'll meet in the morning. But if what I say is true, will you trust me enough to bring your gear back to my apartment? Separate rooms, Tori. Nothing you don't want, I promise.'

'And you'll let me leave?'

'I don't have a choice.'

'No,' she said heavily. 'You don't.'

He was right, her hotel was appalling. They went back to his apartment. Jake slept on the settee. Tori slept in his room.

'I'll spend the night pacing,' he told her when she objected. 'So I might as well pace on the balcony. Once upon a time a man could go through a couple of packets of smokes in this situation. Now it's traffic fumes or nothing.'

She was so tired she hardly smiled. So he made up the settee for himself, and Tori lay in Jake's bed and thought she was so tired she should sleep, but sleep was a long time coming.

The bed was really comfortable and really big. Big enough to entertain?

There'd have been women. Of course there must have been women.

But none of them had stayed very long, she thought. This place was almost clinically austere.

Her little relocatable home had been austere and beige. This place was austere and grey.

Maybe it was chic, but she hated it just the same as she'd hated the drabness of her relocatable. It was cool and grey and impersonal.

She missed her dogs.

The dogs were fine. They'd hardly miss her. But there was no one—nothing—to hug.

There was silence from the sitting room. Maybe Jake wasn't serious about pacing. Maybe he'd said that to make her think he was taking her news seriously—that he thought it was a big deal.

He'd accepted it so smoothly. Maybe it had even happened before.

That was unthinkable.

But why should she lie here and want this baby to be as new and as wonderful an experience for Jake as it was for her?

It couldn't be, she thought. She and her baby would be in Australia. Jake would be here.

She'd organise videos.

Not of the birth, though, she thought hastily. There was no way she was going there. She'd do that on her own.

By herself. There was a bleak thought.

Jet lag was insidious, she decided. Exhaustion was making her depressed, or maybe it was this appalling apartment. Jake had prints on the wall—charcoal sketches of something avant garde. Horrible. In the moonlight she couldn't see detail; she could only see the vague outline of garish figures.

Thinking on, it wasn't even moonlight. It was the glare of a million buildings, lit at night with a million neon signs.

How could she be homesick when she'd been away for less than a week?

No matter; she was. She wanted the dogs. She wanted to hear the birds in the trees outside her window.

She wanted for Jake to be not right through that door and for that door not to be closed.

'Go to sleep,' she told herself firmly, desperately. 'Now.'

Pigs might fly.

Jake had learned from years of being on call to hit the pillow and summon sleep. Self-preservation had taught him the knack. It had never failed him—until now.

He'd never had Tori sleeping right through the wall until now.

He'd never been told he'd be a father until now.

He wanted…

He didn't know what he wanted.

He wanted Tori.

If you made a woman pregnant you married her. It was an old dictum—did it still apply?

She'd already refused him.

He didn't know the first thing about relationships. Where to start?

By taking tomorrow off. Yeah, okay, he thought wryly, good one. It was his rostered day off anyway. Very magnanimous. He could do a quick check-in at the hospital before she woke and then he'd show her New York.

But Monday he had a list longer than his arm, and it was too late to delegate. She'd be on her own then.

He could probably cut it a bit. Get home at a reasonable hour.

To find the little wife waiting for him, with supper served and his slippers warmed?

Tori was right. It was a ludicrous concept. Only it had to be thought of. She had to stay.

Why?

He had a sudden vision of himself, aged about seven. Summer holidays. His mother off with one of her lovers. He in his grandparents' mausoleum of a house on Long Island.

Lonely as hell.

Tori was having his baby, and his kid wasn't going to be lonely. If he was going to be a father, he wanted his kid here, whether Tori agreed or not.

His kid?

He'd never thought of being a father. He'd had such a solitary upbringing; he'd simply expected more of the same.

He'd reacted calmly enough to Tori's news. Or more. He'd been so stunned that all he could feel was concern for Tori. To think past that to fatherhood itself…

He'd have a daughter? A son?

The idea was so overwhelming he couldn't take it in.

He let it swirl for a while, trying to figure things out, but no matter how he looked at it, one thing stood out. This child would *not* have his upbringing. His mother telling lies about his father. His parents continents apart.

She had to stay.

He'd marry the mother of his child.

She slept until ten, and when she woke Jake was standing over her, lean and long and gorgeous, wearing a sleek business suit, a crisp white shirt and a crimson tie. What the…

She glanced from him to the clock—and yelped.

He grinned and set toast on the bedside table, then sat on the side of the bed. It was such a familiar thing to do that she practically yelped again.

'Feel up to breakfast?' he said and smiled, and she thought, This man is the father of my child. That was such a seriously sexy, seriously wonderful thing to think that her toes practically curled.

But what was with the suit?

'You're dressed up, why?' she managed.

'I've been into the hospital so I could clear the rest of the day.'

'I thought you had today off.'

'I don't do off days, but I'm free now. Moving on… You don't look like you have morning sickness,' he said, and she hauled her thoughts back to earth. Or almost back to earth.

'I'm only sick if I move fast.'

'Then don't move fast.'

'I won't.'

He leaned forwards and took the pillows from the spare side of the bed, then wedged them behind her. And there it was again, that blast of caring. And of maleness. And of…want?

Down, girl, she told herself fiercely. You have twenty-four

hours left of this man. There's no use lusting after something—someone—you can't have.

But she was definitely lusting.

He was handing over tea and she had to take it, even though there was suddenly a really big part of her that wanted to fling the tea onto his cool-grey carpet, grab him and haul him back onto his own pillows. He was the father of her baby....

'So have you ever been to New York?' he asked, and she blinked and had a couple of sips of tea and mustered her hormones into some sort of corral. But the boundaries she put around them looked frail. Very frail indeed.

'No,' she managed, and her voice came out a squeak and she had to try again.

'So where have you been?' He handed over toast. Her fingers brushed his and she practically yelped all over again. She had to get herself under control.

'Um, Sydney?' she ventured.

'Is that the furthest?' he demanded, astounded.

'Yeah,' she said, defensive, and then because she didn't want him to think she hadn't travelled because she was a wimp, she told him the rest. 'Mum died when Micki and I were small. Dad had the veterinary practice up and we helped him, after school, every holiday. I thought I might travel for a bit after vet school but by the time I finished, Dad had Parkinson's. Micki's marriage was in trouble and she was in Perth. She couldn't help. If I hadn't stayed Dad would have had to sell up and it'd have broken his heart.' She paused and then added quietly, 'Though if he sold up maybe he'd still be alive.'

'Hey, Tori, don't.' He smiled, coaxing her to let it go. 'You can't beat yourself up over decisions like that. And you're here now,' he said. 'Your first overseas experience. You need to stay for more than a day.'

'No.' The thought terrified her.

'Not necessarily with me.'

'I'd mess with your life,' she said and glanced at the spare side of the bed.

'There's no one.'

'I didn't mean that.'

'Okay, you didn't mean that, but I'm telling you anyway. If you want to sleep in my bed for the next month—'

'No!'

'No?'

'No,' she said, and she sounded desperate but there wasn't anything she could do about it. 'I need to get up now.'

'If you need to sleep, then sleep.'

'If I've only got one day in New York, I'm not sleeping.'

'You should take more.'

'I'm house-training Itsy,' she said. 'I can't take more.'

'Tori…'

'I haven't come to interfere with your life. I've just come to tell you and then to go.'

'I can't see that I can let you go.'

'You don't have a choice,' she said, trying hard to sound firm and sure and confident. Was he planning on locking her up until this baby was born? Ha! She'd thrown him, she thought. She'd had a month to get used to the idea of a baby. He'd had less than a day.

'So I'll get up and you can point me to the Statue of Liberty,' she said, moving right on.

'Is that what you want to see?'

'And the Empire State Building, and Central Park and Tiffany's.'

'Tiffany's?' he said blankly.

'My very favourite movie in the whole world. Don't you just love Audrey Hepburn?'

'Like life itself,' he said promptly, and she giggled and ate a bit of toast and thought, This could be okay. She'd do the tourist thing, maybe they'd meet for dinner tonight; they'd discuss practicalities like just how much access he wanted and how they were going to figure it out, and then she'd head back to Australia and get on with it.

'I'll go put on my walking shoes,' he said.

'You don't have to come with me,' she said, startled. 'I'm guessing you'll already have seen the Statue of Liberty.'

'I might have,' he agreed. 'But she's worth a second look. And to be honest, I've never once been inside Tiffany's.'

CHAPTER TEN

THEY did the Empire State Building. They had to queue for two hours but at the top she gasped and decreed the view was worth every minute. She produced a camera and took the shots every tourist took, but she insisted on having him front and centre.

'This is your town,' she said. 'I'm visiting Jake's Manhattan. This is Jake with the Statue of Liberty in the background. Very nice.'

A tourist offered to take a shot of them together and she beamed. 'That'll be good for later,' she decreed, handing over her camera.

'Later?' He held her tightly as the German gentleman lined up the shot—because holding her close seemed the right thing to do. Also it was a good excuse to keep her near him. He hadn't forgotten how good she felt. His body was reminding him every time she came within touching distance.

He could hardly understand her smile, he thought. She must be jet-lagged. She was facing an uncertain future alone and, here she was, cheerfully soaking up every minute of her two-day visit.

She was gorgeous.

But then… 'This will be a shot of Mummy and Daddy for our baby's first album,' she told him as he held her—and desire gave way to something else entirely, a range of emotions he couldn't begin to understand. But he kept her still, and when he saw the resulting picture he thought no one would know by his fixed smile that he felt as if he'd been punched.

But he did feel as though he'd been punched. No matter how many traffic fumes he'd inhaled last night, he didn't have his head round this.

This lovely, vibrant woman was carrying his baby.

And she was only here until tomorrow.

Would he go to Australia for the birth? He must, he thought, as Tori went back to snapping views. And what if something happened early? A miscarriage. A problem later in the pregnancy? What sort of antenatal care would she get in Combadeen?

How could he let her go back to Australia?

But how could he not? He had no hold on her. They'd had, what, a two-day relationship. There was no way a future could be based on that.

But still…

Still, he didn't know what to think.

Finally viewed out, Tori headed to the elevators. A big guy, overweight and overbearing, barged into the elevator beside Tori and pushed her backwards. He saw Tori's hand instinctively move to protect a bump that wasn't there yet, and he wanted to move his body in between them and thump the guy into the bargain.

He wanted to say, 'That's my kid in there. Watch it.'

More. He wanted to say, 'That's my woman, and I'll thump anyone who touches her.'

Only, of course, he didn't. He was civilised and careful; he was a senior medico with a responsible job; he was someone who taught nonaggressive solutions to his staff when patients were violent.

More. He was a guy who walked alone.

But he still wanted to punch the guy's lights out.

His phone rang while he was thinking of it. He answered it as he always did.

'Dr. Hunter?'

'Speaking.'

'Jancey Ian? Her intrathecal catheter's packed up.'

He paused as the rest of the elevator streamed out around them. Swearing under his breath.

Jancey was a tiny African-American woman in her mid-seventies and she had advanced bone metastases. He'd inserted morphine and local anaesthetic via an intrathecal catheter to stop pain that had been almost unbearable.

But not only did Jancey have crumbling vertebrae from the cancer, she also had severe arthritis. It had taken skill, experience and luck to get the drugs flowing to just the right spot. It'd be a miracle if any of the junior doctors on duty could get the catheter back in.

'Level of pain?' he asked, knowing already what the answer would be.

'Bad.' Mardi Fry was the senior nurse on the ward. If she said *bad* it must be hellish.

'I can't…'

'You can.' Tori was suddenly in front of him, facing him down. She'd only heard his side of the conversation, but obviously she'd guessed the rest. 'I'm an unexpected and un-invited guest, and I'm a very happy tourist. Don't you dare leave someone in pain because of me. I'll take a cab to Central Park. Meet me there if you can.'

'Tori…'

'Strawberry Fields at two o'clock,' she said, heading to the cab rank already and calling back over her shoulder. 'That's the bit I most want to see in Central Park. Or back at your apartment at six.'

And she was gone before he could even argue.

* * *

She was asleep when he found her, right where she'd said she'd be, in Central Park, snoozing on a bench in the weak autumn sunlight, with a bag of uneaten bagels on her knee. He touched her on the shoulder and she opened her eyes and smiled at him.

He thought back to the number of dates he'd had to interrupt for medical necessity. There'd always been reproof. But Tori was smiling at him as if this was a whole new date.

'Hey, it's only two o'clock,' she said. 'Well done. All fixed?'

'Piece of cake,' he said. 'Catheter went in like a dream.' In fact, it had been a nightmare, but it was okay now. Jancey was out of pain and asleep.

She searched his face, and he thought she saw the truth, but she said nothing. No recriminations. No questions

A woman in a million.

'So what were you dreaming of?' he asked.

'Names.'

'Names?'

'Baby names,' she said, as if he was a little bit thick. 'For some reason now I'm in Strawberry Fields I'm thinking Jude. But I'm also thinking maybe Elizabeth for my mother?'

'You don't sound sure.'

'And why would I be sure? This baby's the size of a peanut, and do you know how many books there are on children's names? If you help me we'll barely get through them.'

'Do you want me to help?'

There was a moment's silence, and then, carefully, as if she was bestowing a huge honour on him, she broke her bagel in half.

'Share,' she said. 'That's why I'm here. Though I have to say if your mother was Gertie it's not going to happen.'

'It's not, but I don't think I want anyone called after my mother anyway.'

'That's right, she was a horror,' Tori said cheerfully,

bestowing his parentage the attention it deserved. Which in itself was strangely healing. 'That makes life easier. Can we go to Tiffany's now?'

So they went to Tiffany's, a place Jake had never been to. Yes, it was famous, but it was definitely a girl place. He felt like waiting outside, only then he couldn't watch Tori enjoy herself, which was growing more and more unthinkable.

So in he went. The doorman welcomed them and the unobtrusive staff watched with indulgent eyes. Of all the women in here Tori stood out. She was a woman with no rings on her fingers, nothing, no jewellery at all.

But Tori wasn't looking at anything she might buy. She was intent on the fantasy.

'Oh, wow,' she breathed, as she reached a display case of tiaras that must be worth a king's ransom. Or several kings' ransoms, he thought, as he checked out the prices.

'Aren't they wonderful,' Tori said, giggling. 'What if you were wearing it and it fell off in the mud?'

'I don't think there's any mud where any of these are going.'

'No,' she said, suddenly disapproving. 'They'll be worn once a year, maybe, twice tops, and the rest of the time they'll be stuck in a safe. There they'll just sit until something like the fire happens, and what a waste.'

She had a different perspective, he thought, as he watched her move from jewel to jewel. She was loving looking at these beautiful things, but there was no wistfulness in her eyes at all.

She'd lost everything, and yet she wanted nothing.

'Look at this,' she breathed, and he looked more closely and was as stunned as she was.

It was the most amazing ring he'd ever seen. Its centre was a diamond, perfectly cut as a heart, and so large it took his breath away. Every facet glistened and sparkled. On the outer edge of the heart were five rubies, set into white gold to glitter at each extremity. Surrounding them was a ring of smaller diamonds; though, thinking on, they were only small in comparison to the central stone.

The ring was ostentatious and it was ridiculous and it'd take more muscle than most women had in their ring finger to wear it without complaint—but for all that it was quite extraordinarily lovely. And it didn't even have a price tag.

'Oh, wow,' Tori breathed. 'What a knuckle duster.' She giggled again—and then she looked sideways at it. 'You know, it's like something absolutely exquisite, but blown up,' she said slowly. 'A little version would be just perfect, but this… It's wonderful but it's crazy.'

'You'd never want something like this.'

'Are you kidding?' Again came that infectious chuckle. 'What's not to want? Mind, I'd have to find me a sheikh, and sheikhs are in small supply where I come from.'

'Do you have any jewellery at all?' he asked, but almost as the words left his mouth he knew he shouldn't have asked. She'd been working when the fire came through. Nothing had been saved.

Toby, the erstwhile fiancé, had a lot to answer for. Again, Jake found himself dealing with anger.

But the fire was history. Tori had moved on and so should he. And luckily Tori hadn't heard the question. Her attention was caught yet again.

'Oh…'

She was peering into a different display section now, where opulence had given way to a far more demure kind of beauty. She seemed totally captivated, not amused this time, but rather stunned.

She was gazing at a Celtic love knot, wrought in gold with silver threads woven through. Compared to the jewellery they'd just looked at, this was tiny, but it was no less beautiful. Slivers of diamond were scattered through the knot, like stones set into rope. It looked rough, almost as though it had been hewn from the earth already formed. It hung on a simple silver chain, and Jake looked at it and then looked at Tori, and her eyes were shining with unshed tears.

'It's like my mother's,' she whispered. 'It's not the same but it's so close. She wore it always. And it was burned.' She managed a watery smile. 'I need to buy it,' she said simply, and an assistant was sliding it out of the display case before she finished speaking.

Tori reached to touch it with hands that trembled. She ran her fingers across its intricate surface, almost reverently.

'I'll take it,' she said and she hadn't even looked at the price.

'Tori…'

She was hardly aware of him. This chain had been a part of her past that was somehow being restored, Jake thought, as he watched her face, and he was feeling just a bit emotional himself. And he knew what he wanted to do. He'd been thinking it ever since he'd walked into the place, and now was the right time.

'Will you let me?' he asked, and he laid his hand over hers. 'It would be my honour and my pleasure—and my pride as well—to buy this for you.'

She turned, puzzled. 'Why?'

'You're the mother of my baby,' he said simply and surely. In truth there were many emotions at play here, and the fact that Tori was pregnant was only a tiny part of the whole, but it was all he could understand right now.

'I need to do something to mark this,' he said softly, though the assistant had melted discreetly away. 'It's a piece of jewellery that reminds you of what's lost. Can it also be something to mark what's to come?'

She looked up at him then through a mist of tears. She gave a wavering smile—and she sniffed. Oh, for heaven's sake, he was feeling teary himself. Whoa, that wasn't going to happen. What was this woman doing to him?

He got practical by handing over a handkerchief. Distracted, she gazed down at it in disbelief. 'A handkerchief?'

'What's wrong with a handkerchief?'

'Guys do this in romance novels,' she said faintly. 'Not in real life. What sort of modern male carries handkerchiefs?'

'Men who get their laundry done?' But she wasn't listening. She was buying time, he thought, fighting to get her emotions in order. She turned her back on him and blew her nose, and when she turned back she had her face straight— or almost. Her eyes were still shimmering.

How had he ever thought she was plain? he wondered. She was quite extraordinarily beautiful.

He wanted her. He wanted her so badly....

'But I can...I can afford it,' she said breathlessly. 'Easily. There's no need for you to pay.'

'I know that, but still...will you grant me the honour of buying it for you.'

'There you go again,' she said darkly. 'Romance novels have a lot to answer for. If I didn't know you made such a lousy five-minute dater I'd suspect you'd been taking chivalry lessons.'

'No lessons,' he said. 'Put it on.' He lifted it from the velvet and held it out.

Silently she turned so he could fasten it around her neck. He clipped the hook closed, and then, because the temptation was irresistible, he bent and kissed her, lightly on the nape of her neck. Her skin felt smooth and lovely, and for an instant...for just an instant, he felt her lean into him, let herself relax against him, trust him.

'Jake...'

He wanted to kiss her properly, as he needed to kiss her, as she deserved to be kissed, but her moment of weakness was gone. She tugged away, apparently to look in the mirror, but he knew it was more than that. He'd felt her body stiffen.

He'd felt her fear.

Bad move, he thought. Very bad move, considering what he was thinking.

The assistant had melted away again in the emotional stuff—how did they know to do that?—but as Tori moved to the mirror she materialised again, beaming her approval.

'Will madam take it?'

'Madam's taking it,' Tori said softly, and a slight tremor ran through her, a tremor she couldn't disguise. 'Madam fell in love with romance novels when she was thirteen years old and she knows when she's hooked.'

'Does this mean you'll let me buy it for you?' Jake asked.

'Why yes,' she said softly. 'Yes, I believe it does.'

They bought Chinese takeaway and took it back to the apartment for dinner because Tori was simply too tired to go on.

Jake usually ate at his kitchen bench. His dining table was covered in journals, half-written papers, important work in progress.

He could sort it and stack it neatly, he thought, but that could take half an hour. Or he could make Tori eat at the kitchen bench.

But if this was the only night he had to persuade her, then he needed to move fast. So he cleared the table by the simple expedient of tipping it lengthways. It worked a treat. Hey, when was the last time he'd seen this table? It had cost him a bomb. It was a great table.

Or maybe not, he conceded, thinking on. The table was of cool-grey lacquer, designed to match the apartment's cool-grey walls. He remembered Tori's scathing comments about grey. Hmm.

Tori was looking at the mess as they ate, bemused. 'It'll take you days to get that back in order.'

'I have days.' He'd have all the time in the world after she went home, he thought. *If* she went home.

How to broach it again?

He didn't for a while. They shared their food. They both had soda—he'd have liked a beer but Jancey's catheter might mean he'd be called out again. They listened to music. She liked his music. That was something the decorator hadn't chosen.

'What time's your plane tomorrow?' he asked.

'Late afternoon. I figure I'll sleep in.'

'No more sightseeing?'

'I hear Soho's good,' she said. 'But maybe not. You need to go to work, right?'

He did. He'd been trying to figure out how not to need to go to work, but case lists for Monday were always the most complex. If he cancelled, patients would be sent home.

'You can't let them down,' Tori said softly, and he knew she understood.

He was doing a rapid assessment of cases in his head but it wasn't helping. He'd seen Jack Carver in the cardiac ward on Friday. Jack had severe ulceration on his legs, so severe amputation was becoming an option. He needed shunts to restore blood supply back so they could heal, but he had a cardiac condition and diabetic complications as well. When Jake had done the initial assessment—something he usually avoided but he seemed to be doing it more in the weeks since he'd met Tori—Jack's wife had been holding her husband's hand as though if she let go he'd drown.

'Please,' she'd said to him. 'Jack's all I have. Make him well.'

The risk of Jack losing his leg—or worse—was increasing every day he waited. He couldn't reschedule, Jake thought grimly. No matter what he wanted personally, he needed to be there tomorrow.

And Jancey would be watching the door, waiting for him. He couldn't let Jancey down.

'I could have done with some warning of your visit,' he growled, but Tori shook her head.

'I suspect you'd still be as busy even if you were expecting me, and I didn't want to interrupt your life. I *don't* want to interrupt your life. Soho will just be shops. I might go on my own or I might just sleep, but either way, I can take a cab to the airport. I don't need your company.'

But her voice wobbled a little at that, and he noticed her fingers crept to the chain at her throat.

'You should stay,' he said strongly.

'I need to go home. I need to start my life as I need to go on.'

'Why not stay here?'

'We already talked about that.'

'I'd like to marry you.'

There was a sharp intake of breath. But… 'You've said that before,' she whispered, still touching her chain. 'Just because I'm having your baby, it doesn't make it any better.'

'I think I love you.'

She gazed across the table at him, seemingly bemused. Seemingly astounded. 'You think?'

'I don't know,' he admitted. 'Hell, Tori, I haven't done this before.'

'Done what?'

'Become involved.'

'You sound like it's happened against your will.'

'Well, what do you think?' he said, raking his hair. 'I don't have a clue how I'm feeling. But we're going to be parents. You need to rebuild anyway. You've lost everything.…'

And finally she reacted with something apart from shock. 'I haven't lost everything,' she retorted, and she tilted her chin and met his gaze levelly and calmly.

'Okay, you've got your dogs,' he conceded.

'I've got my home.'

'A relocatable.'

'I have my community.' The emotion now was suddenly pure, unmitigated anger. 'I have my work,' she said, struggling to stay calm. 'You have your work, too. It's important, as my work's important. But I have more. I have *place*. My parents lived and worked at Combadeen and so do I. I know every family rebuilding on the ridge. My parents are buried in the Combadeen cemetery. I've buried my dogs behind our house. Okay, I've been stunned, shocked, gutted by the fires and their aftermath but I'm handling it. And I'm moving on to make a home for myself, in my place, not in some sterile, grey, designer shoebox on the seventeenth floor of a thirty storey tower block.'

'It's not—'

'A shoebox? Yes, it is,' she retorted. 'They're all shoeboxes. It's what's around them that matters, and what's in them. Here, you'd be at work all day every day, and the shoebox would close in on me.'

'You could work part-time. We could get somewhere a bit bigger. Hell, Tori, you need looking after.'

'I don't need looking after.'

'You're pregnant.'

'And I still don't need looking after.' Her anger was building rather than subsiding. 'I have a community who cares. I have friends and I have colleagues. You've seen me at a point where I was at my lowest, where the resources of the whole district were stretched to the limit, but don't judge me on that. Don't judge Combadeen by that. There's not one person in Combadeen who'd suggest I live in a grey monument to solitude and go crazy!'

'You wouldn't go crazy.'

'I would if I lived here,' she said, rising and glowering. 'So would you, but you don't live here either. You use it to crash or to study or to take a shower. No one lives in places like this. Living… Jake, you don't know what living is, and I'm surely not raising my child teaching him this life is normal.'

She closed her eyes then, and she swayed. He was on his feet in an instant, surging around the table to hold her, but her eyes snapped open and she stepped away.

'No,' she said. 'Don't.'

'Don't?'

'Don't touch me,' she whispered. 'I was a fool to come. The truth was I wanted to see you, as well as needing to tell you about our baby, but it was wrong. You and me… No. There's no you and me.'

'Tori…'

'You're alone,' she whispered. 'And that's the way you want it. But if I'm alone I'd curl up and die. I need people. I need dogs. I need…life.'

She sighed then and steadied.

'I'm sorry, Jake,' she said. 'Getting angry was dumb. Yelling at you is dumb. You're doing the best you can.' She shook her head as if clearing fog. 'Okay, here's confession time,' she said. 'I'm trying desperately not to fall in love with you. You say you might love me? Well, maybe I know that I could love you. And you know what that means? If I came here, then you'd risk me clinging.'

He didn't understand. 'Why would you cling? You have your work.'

'I'm not talking about my work. I'm talking about needing you, and you needing me. You're fine with the idea of looking after me. Could you ever admit that *you* need *me*?'

'I…' There was deathly silence.

'No,' she said, and she was fighting now for the composure she'd lost. 'Enough. This is dumb talk, and we both know it. We're two mature professionals—we can handle this. Your work is waiting, and my life is waiting. So please, Jake…'

She took a deep breath. 'Please, Jake,' she said again. 'I'm exhausted and I need to go to bed. Thank you for a wonderful day.' Her fingers crept once again to her Celtic knot. 'Thank you for my chain. I'll keep it for ever. But now…' Another deep breath.

'Now I'm going into your bedroom,' she said softly, steadying. 'And I'm going to bed. Alone. That's the way it has to be. We both know that. I guess when I wake up in the morning you'll be gone to work. So I'll get on my plane tomorrow and I won't look back. Yes, you'll want to see our baby. We can work that out later. But we need to do it in a way where I can be normal and civil, and the fact that I had the best night of my life with you, and I'm thinking entirely inappropriate thoughts, can be forgotten. Please, Jake, that's what I need. So goodnight.'

And before he could guess what she intended, she took three swift steps towards him. She took his face in her hands and she kissed him, fast and hard, on the mouth. Then, before he had a chance to respond, before he could hold her as he needed to hold her, she pushed herself away.

'Goodnight, Jake,' she said, firmly and steadily. 'And goodbye.'

And she was gone, into his bedroom, closing the door firmly behind her.

And he knew he couldn't follow.

It was all very well being angry and virtuous and sure. Anger and virtue and certainty lasted all the way until the door was shut, and then she just felt miserable.

Nothing else. Just plain bad.

He'd asked her to marry him and she'd refused.

She'd hardly had a choice, she told herself, fighting to drum up anger again.

What had she hoped for?

And there was the crux. The biggie. Hope. Finally she was acknowledging exactly what she'd hoped for.

She loved him. She'd told herself that one night together was simply a way of moving on, but it was so much more, and that was regardless of her pregnancy. He'd said he thought he loved her but he didn't know what it meant.

Love.

She thought back to Jake holding her as they'd buried a little koala named Manya. She thought of the way he'd held Glenda's hand, of the way he'd laughed at Bitsy.

She thought of Jake in the ward, talking through a procedure to the patient he was about to anaesthetise, carefully so there could be no misunderstanding. She knew he'd be wonderful.

She thought of the way Jake's body felt against hers.

'Oh, enough, you're behaving like a moonstruck teenager,' she scolded herself. 'You've come all this way and he's been lovely. He's taken you sightseeing. He's given you a beautiful piece of jewellery. He's reacted to our baby with honour. He even tried to figure out how he could love you. What else do you want from the man?'

Nothing.

Jake lay on the too-hard settee and stared up at his blank ceiling. Running the conversation over and over in his head.

Love…

Yes, he'd said it, but Tori had known he hadn't meant it and she must be right. Love would be something you learned over months or, more probably, years, a gradual build-up of trust and affection. It surely wasn't what he and Tori had. A one-and-a-half-minute date, followed by one night of passion.

Unbidden, the words of his mother crept back into his subconscious.

'I fell in love with your father on one meeting. One meeting! How ridiculous was that? He carted me off to some strange country, to a life I had no way of dealing with, and look what happened. Love at first sight? Don't make me laugh.'

Nothing made sense. The night was too long, the settee was too hard, the concept of love and of home was too difficult to get his head around.

That Tori could say she loved him, that she could possibly throw her heart where her head should be, seemed unreal. And if she felt like that, then why wouldn't she marry him?

Should he have insisted he love her? Do the romantic-hero thing?

If he did that he'd be no better than his father.

But he no longer believed in his father as the villain. He no longer knew what he believed in. He was getting into territory that was simply too hard.

And the hardest thing…

The hardest thing was that Tori was right through that door. His woman.

She wasn't his woman. He had no rights.

She felt like his woman.

'So what are you intending, caveman?' he muttered into the night. 'Go and stake your claim? You've done enough damage. You have a surgical list longer than your arm waiting for you in the morning. It's not fair on your patients if you don't sleep.'

Somehow he managed to switch off, and sleep.

But he couldn't turn off his dreams.

She woke and she knew he'd gone. The cool-grey apartment practically echoed.

She'd thought—maybe she'd hoped—that she'd wake when he left and she could say goodbye, but it had been

almost dawn before she'd drifted into troubled sleep. Her exhausted body had finally demanded what it needed and Jake's
bedside clock was telling her it was eight o'clock.

She threw back the covers and padded out to the living
room, cautiously, just to see, but the sleek leather settee was
back being a sleek leather settee. The spare bedding was
neatly folded, ready to be stored back in the bedroom closet.

There was a note on the bench.

Catheter trouble again. Travel safe. I'll be in touch.

A farewell note. How romantic. She crumpled it and slid
it into the trash.

The kitchenette was squeaky clean, not even a dirty coffee
mug to tell her he'd breakfasted before he'd left. She touched
the designer kettle. It was cold. Really cold. He hadn't even
had coffee here.

If she lived here she wouldn't have her morning coffee
here either, she decided. This place was awful.

He'd come home tonight to this, she thought, feeling
more dismal by the minute as the cool of the apartment—
and the lack of Jake—soaked into her. She'd have changed
the sheets and put hers in the commercial laundry basket
she'd seen near the entrance. Maybe by the time Jake got
home the laundry would already have been collected,
cleaned and returned.

Nothing would remain of her visit.

There should be something.

Stupid or not, she wanted there to be something.

Her fingers moved instinctively to her throat, to her chain,
to something she knew she'd treasure for ever. She loved her
chain. She loved that Jake had given it to her. She should have
refused—but how strong could a woman be?

Not strong enough.

'I should leave him something,' she said, gazing helplessly
around at the designer chic. 'I can't leave him with grey.'

And then a thought.

'I did it for me,' she murmured to herself. 'How hard would it be in New York?

'Soho maybe?

'I'd need a cab. Maybe I'd need two.

'I'd also need time.

'So what are you waiting for?' she demanded of herself. 'Jake wanted me to make a home here. Maybe I can do that, only not quite the way he imagined.'

He knew when her plane took off for he'd checked the Qantas® web site. In truth he checked it half a dozen times, and if he hadn't been pushed to his limit with his surgical list maybe he'd have cracked and headed to the airport. 'Just to say goodbye,' he told himself and wondered why he had to tell himself that. Surely it was obvious.

But the hands of the clock slipped inexorably around and six o'clock was suddenly right there.

'Not quite ready to knock off yet,' said the surgeon he was working with, and Jake thought, How bad did he have it? How often had he glanced up at the clock on the operating room wall?

He didn't have it bad. It was only…

It was only that it was now one minute past six. The plane would be taxiing to the runway.

Tori was gone.

She could see the Statue of Liberty from the plane, lit up and beautiful.

She sniffed and the man in the seat next to her smiled in sympathy and handed over a tissue.

'Thank you,' she managed and sniffed again and groped in her purse. 'It's very nice of you but I have a handkerchief.'

* * *

It was one in the morning before Jake finally finished. He was wrecked, emotionally and physically, and by the time he reached his apartment his legs didn't want to work any more.

He worked out in the basement gym most mornings. He hadn't this morning. One lost workout and his legs were turning to jelly.

Or maybe it was because of one lost Tori.

'See, that's what you can't think,' he told himself. 'That kind of thinking does no one any good.'

But he rode the elevator and he thought those kinds of thoughts all the way up.

How soon could he go to Australia?

What use was going to Australia? He belonged here. Here was home.

Home. He turned the key in the lock and thought it was no such thing. It was grey.

He was starting to feel ill. He'd had Tori here and he'd let her go. Leaving him with grey.

He pushed the door wide and it was anything but.

It was decorated by Tori.

It might not be the same stuff she'd bought in Melbourne but it was as close as made no difference. Back in Australia she'd transformed a beige relocatable home into a riot of colour and life.

Here it was—a riot.

Colours, colours and more colours. Cushions, lamps, throws, vases, prints, weird and wonderful statues, a Persian carpet almost completely covering the cool grey tiles, an imitation log fire!

It was too much. It was…wonderful.

He found himself smiling, moving through the room, fingering things that were tactile as well as lovely. It was warm, inviting and wonderful.

His table had been moved against the wall. It was covered

with a rich tapestry, and a vast mirror set behind it so it reflected the warmth of the lamps.

There was an antique desk against the far wall. The books he'd swept onto the floor last night were neatly stacked, ready to be used again.

And then...

A faint noise had him moving to the bedroom. He opened the door and a small brown cat stalked out, looking suspicious and curious and eager, all at once. A half-grown cat, fawn with a tip of white on its tail.

It was followed by another brown cat, even smaller, but this one had no tip.

Burmese? He wasn't sure of his cats. They looked like Siamese cats, he thought, only different.

The first one sniffed his shoes, then carefully wound its way round and round his ankles.

The second one sat and watched, acting superior.

Cats...

There was a note on his bed—on top of the riot of an amazing patchwork quilt.

I looked for another Celtic love knot but couldn't find one. These are my alternative. Meet Ferdy and Freddy. They're from the pet store on the note stuck on their litter tray. I paid double their asking price on condition that if you really don't want them they'll take them back. But I'd recommend keeping them. They keep each other company all day and when you get home...well, they might just mean you do come home.

He found himself grinning. Ferdy and Freddy.

Ferdy—or was it Freddy?—yowled. His brother joined

in, then both of them set their tails high and stalked over to the fridge.

What was he supposed to do with cats?

Bemused, he opened the fridge, and found what he was supposed to do with cats. Tori had thought of everything.

'You'll have to go back,' he told them as he fed them, but he couldn't do it tonight.

When would he find time to take them back tomorrow?

He had work to do before he went to bed. There was a case he needed to look up for the next day.

He sat down at his new desk and opened a textbook.

Ferdy was on his knee in seconds, followed by Freddy.

How was a man supposed to work when he was...when he was home?

Where was Tori right now? Somewhere around Hawaii?

Not that far.

Too far.

This place was wonderful.

It was missing something.

'I don't think I can,' he told the cats, fondling two ears. Fondling four ears.

'Impossible. My work is here.

'Yes, but...

'She's just given me two more complications.

'I can handle complications.'

He couldn't, though, he thought, or not immediately. It'd take some thought.

'Love takes time,' he told the cats. 'Months. Maybe years.'

Years didn't bear thinking of.

He closed his eyes. This was crazy. He was a man who walked alone.

Ferdy dug his claws into his thigh and gently kneaded.

'I don't do pets,' he said through gritted teeth. 'I don't do…love?'

He had this all the wrong way round. He'd go to sleep and he'd wake up in the morning being sensible.

Maybe, or maybe not.

CHAPTER ELEVEN

THE operation on Harley had been long and perilous. The big schnauzer was only seven years old, but the liver abscess he'd developed was as unexpected as it was lethal and the only option if he was to survive was to remove part of the liver.

At least Tori was no longer working by herself. Her new workplace had specialist canine surgeons. She'd been able to call for help, and then work as the assistant of a far more experienced surgeon.

All the same, she was exhausted.

She should be feeling perky and full of energy at five months pregnant, she told herself, but it wasn't happening. Try as she might, she couldn't be perky. Ever since she'd come back from New York—okay, even before that, ever since Jake left, she conceded—there'd been something exhausting her that wasn't pregnancy. Something was trying to tug her back into the grey fog she'd been in after the fire.

And she wasn't going to be tugged, she told herself fiercely as she worked. She had great friends, a lovely new job, caring colleagues; she'd just saved Harley, and Rusty and Itsy were waiting for her back home. Doreen and Glenda cared for the dogs during the day, but the dogs knew who their mistress was and when Tori arrived they almost turned inside out with joy.

They'd be expecting her now. Tori glanced at her watch and winced. She still needed to talk to Harley's owners, and stop off and buy something for tea, and then collect the dogs…and the tiredness was insidious.

Two more days 'til the weekend, she promised herself, two more days until she could spend the whole time at home. But the weekend brought more problems. Most of the population of the relocatable village spent their weekends up on the ridge, working on their new homes, but for some reason her head still wouldn't let her go there. And there was the other thing. At the weekend she had time to think of Jake.

The surgeon was closing. 'It's as good as we can get,' he told her. 'You want to go tell Harley's mum and dad the good news?'

Of course she did. She pinned on a bright smile and opened the door—and Jake was in the waiting room.

He was reading a copy of *Horse & Hound*, as though it was totally riveting.

Harley's owners, an elderly couple who'd been frantic about their dog, sprang to their feet. Jake gave her a tiny smile, acknowledging her priorities, and retreated again to his horses. Or hounds.

'Hi,' Tori said, as much to him as to Paul and Ida Clemens, and then somehow forced herself back to professional mode. 'It's okay,' she told them quickly. 'More than okay. It's good. We've taken about twenty percent of the liver but that includes a wide margin of healthy tissue. We're sure we have it all. As long as we can keep his cholesterol under control there's no reason why he shouldn't live happily into a ripe old age.'

The elderly couple stared at her in silence for a long moment—and then Paul put his hands on his face and sank back into his chair. The elderly farmer's shoulders shook with silent sobs. His wife sat down and hugged him. Tori produced a box of tissues and Paul grabbed about a dozen.

He needed them all.

They waited then, all of them, for Paul to recover. Tori was achingly aware of Jake watching from the sidelines, but she couldn't hurry this. Paul and Ida had lost their farm in the fires. They'd barely survived by holding blankets over their heads as they lay in shallows of their dam. Harley had been under the blankets with them.

If they needed time, she'd give them all the time in the world.

Finally Paul had himself under control—or almost. He sat while Ida held his hand, and while Tori gently repeated the good news. Then their questions started. She repeated the initial diagnosis. Hypercholesterolemia—massively elevated cholesterol—had caused the liver abscess. Schnauzers were genetically prone to it, and of course Paul and Ida had treated Harley as a human before the fires, and afterwards they could refuse his pleading eyes nothing. So Harley had eaten cheese and sausages and chocolate, and finally his liver had started to disintegrate under the strain.

'So you think you can resist now?' Tori asked them, and Ida managed a strained smile.

'Once upon a time we were firm parents,' she said. 'We can go back to that. Can't we, Paul?'

'I guess…'

'And we move into our new home next week.' Ida was sounding firmer, ready to move on. 'We'll be able to take Harley home to somewhere permanent.'

'No chocolate?' Paul said.

'No chocolate,' Ida said and looked speculatively at Paul's rotund girth. 'I have the men in my life back, and I'm not risking anything again, thank you very much. Can we see him?'

'Of course you can. Our nurse will be taking him through into recovery,' Tori said—and they thanked her and Tori was left with Jake. He put down *Horse & Hound*.

'Hi,' she managed finally, but it didn't come out properly. 'Um, why are you here?'

'You're supposed to say, "Welcome."'

'You're very welcome,' she said, and he was. Could he feel it, she wondered. Just how welcome he was?

'I was hoping for five minutes of your time.'

'Five minutes?'

'All the best dates are five minutes,' he said. 'You can meet the love of your life in five minutes. Or, as it happens, in one and a half minutes if you try hard enough.'

There was enough in that to take her breath away. It did take her breath away. She wanted to sink onto the seat Paul had just vacated and maybe hyperventilate.

Where was a paper bag when she needed one?

'So Harley really will be okay?' he asked, giving her time to recover, and she thought she could do this; she could talk medicine until she got herself coherent. Maybe.

'It was a beautiful resection of the liver,' she managed. 'Textbook case. Guy Saller's our surgeon—he's the best.'

'So you didn't do it.'

'I don't have the skills.'

'You tried antibiotics and closed drainage first?' He was definitely giving her time.

'We tried everything. I know, resection's last-resort stuff, but believe me, this was last resort. If we'd waited any longer we risked rupture. He's young and healthy. The liver has every chance of regenerating, and best of all he's abstained from alcohol so cirrhosis isn't a problem.'

'You checked for cirrhosis?' he said faintly.

'It's happened,' she said, recovering enough now to start to smile. 'Ida and Paul have given him everything else—why not a wee drop of sherry with theirs at night?'

'You're kidding me.'

'I've seen cases of alcoholic poisoning in dogs,' she told

him. 'The stupidity of owners sometimes defies belief. Jake, why are you here?' And then as he didn't answer straight-away, she jumped in for him. 'Is there a problem at the lodge?'

'There's no problem.'

'Do you need to sign papers for sale or something? Rob tells me the farmhouse had been cleaned up and is looking great.'

'That's what I'd like to talk to you about.'

'It is?'

'It is,' he said. 'So about that five minutes…'

'You've already had it,' she said, but she couldn't get her voice to work properly again. She was sounding breathless.

She was feeling breathless.

'Nope,' he said. 'The five-minute date has to start at a des-ignated place. The first date was in a booth in the Combadeen Hall. Our second date has to be somewhere else. I have a rental car outside. Can I take you to my designated date spot?'

'Your designated date spot,' she said, faintly.

'It's not so far.'

'I need to collect the dogs.'

'I dropped in on Glenda and Doreen,' he said, and at the look on her face he grinned. 'I had to do something. I landed five hours ago—I made a beeline for you, only to be told you were in surgery and weren't expected out until now. Unlike Manhattan Central, there's a dearth of people to talk to. Even Paul and Ida had taken themselves off to stay with their daughter, and *Horse & Hound* circa 1997 has a limited appeal. So I've heard all about how Glenda's hand is now behaving beautifully and how well Doreen is. I've been slob-bered on by one vast golden retriever—what are you feeding her by the way? I thought she was supposed to be a runt. Oh, and I've bought Bitsy.'

'You've bought Bitsy.' She was suddenly feeling faint.

'I wanted him,' Jake said. 'I've wanted him for months. Like some other things I've wanted. I've been telling myself I was stupid, but a man can only do that for so long before he starts believing it and starts to act stupid. So I've been to see the breeder, and yes, she kept him for herself, but money talks, and I can pick him up as soon as I'm ready. There're just a couple of things I need to sort first.' He hesitated. 'No. There's only one thing. One really important thing. Five minutes, Tori. Will you come with me and listen?'

'I don't think…'

'No, don't think,' he said. 'Thinking does your head in. I've been thinking and thinking and it's doing me no good at all. And finally…you know what? I stopped thinking and I'm letting my heart decide.'

They drove in silence, past the lodge, through the burned-out state forest and up onto the ridge.

The year had been kind, with above average rainfall and gentle weather, and the Australian bush had regenerated as only the Australian bush can. Burned trees had new shoots spurting manically out of blackened trunks. Grasses and ferns had pushed up through the ashes. It still looked dreadfully scarred; there were places where the heat had been so intense that it'd take years to come back, but it was no longer grey.

And rebuilding had begun in earnest. Every second house site had been cleared of debris and was now a half-built home. With the kinder weather many families had brought caravans up to the ridge so they could live close to where they were rebuilding.

There were birds back as well, and as they drove there were wallabies feeding on the roadside. As dusk settled Tori could almost imagine the fire had never been.

But it had. Her life would never be the same.

If the fire hadn't happened…she wouldn't have met Jake.

She wouldn't be pregnant—and her hand touched her tummy as it did a hundred times a day.

'Thank you for sending me the ultrasound pictures,' Jake said gravely, and she thought he must have seen the movement. Self-consciously she linked her hands onto her knees and stared straight ahead.

She would not think about why he was here, she decided. She would not.

She would not allow herself to hope.

'Did you like them?' she asked. 'I carry mine in my purse.'

'I carry mine in my wallet,' he said, and she gasped.

'You're joking.'

'My kid,' he said gravely. 'My wallet.' He smiled. 'By the way, I checked every picture and not one of them's taken from the right angle. Do we know if we have a daughter or a son?'

We. The tiny word was enough to make her breathless all over again. She had to fight to make herself speak.

'I didn't want to know,' she managed at last. 'I like surprises.'

'Like me coming?'

'I'm not sure what to think about you coming.'

'Don't think,' he said again. 'Just feel. It's the only safe way.'

There was nothing she could say to that, so she sat in silence until they pulled up at their destination. Which was his farmhouse—her former wildlife shelter—only it was very different from when she'd left it.

As a child she remembered this place looking beautiful, when the doctor and his wife had loved it. But it had only ever been a weekend retreat for them. Jake's father been on call all the time, and he'd lived in Combadeen, so maybe it had been shabby even then.

Now it was anything but shabby. It was a magnificent homestead, its weatherboards gleaming with fresh white paint, its gracious verandah running the full circle of the house, the ancient river-gum timbers of the decking rubbed and oiled back to their original glory.

Someone had worked in the garden. There were so many roses that possums could come and share, she thought, and there'd still be enough to go around.

The French windows were cleaned and gleaming. Some of them were open, and there were soft white drapes floating out in the warm evening breeze.

It looked…like home, she thought, stunned, as Jake helped her out of the car. She didn't need help but she was so dazed she accepted it anyway and she didn't object as he led her into the house and took her from room to room without saying a word.

Why was she here? Why was he here?

It was so beautiful.

It wasn't furnished yet. The rooms were bare. The place was a home waiting for its people. Dogs, she thought suddenly, and kids, and her hand touched her tummy again before she could help herself.

'There's something else you need to see before I explain myself,' Jake said softly, and she opened her mouth to argue—or ask, or something—but she couldn't think what to argue or ask or something so she closed it again. He took her hand and led her and she let herself be led.

Out of the house. Back to the car, then along the track, and into the first driveway on the left.

Home. Or home as she'd once known it. Now it was a mass of regenerating bushland. All that was left was the chimney. The hearth, the fireplace, the heart of the home for her parents' lives, for her grandparents' lives, stretching far, far back…

Now the scene for grief and destruction.

Only she wasn't feeling grief now, or not so much. It was tempered by this new little life inside her. It was tempered by her dogs, her new job, her new life.

It was tempered by Jake's hand.

Once again he was helping her out of the car. He was leading her along the path to where the house had once been, then stopping by the ancient lemon tree that had somehow miraculously survived. Its singed branches had re-generated, and amazingly it was loaded with lemons. The sight actually made her smile.

A massive gum had fallen right in front of it. The team of men who'd cleared the place had taken away the smaller litter but they'd chopped the log into three, obviously thinking she might want to use it. For landscaping or something.

She couldn't think of using anything here.

But Jake had brought along a rug. He spread it across the log so any soot was covered and he propelled her gently downwards.

'Sit,' he said, and she sat because she was beyond arguing.

Then, 'I've done all I can without your input,' he told her. 'It's time I brought you onboard.'

'Onboard?'

'Onto my sea of plans,' he said. 'I have three directions I can go, and I don't know which one to take.'

'I don't understand.'

'Okay,' he said gently and he sat down beside her. He took her hand in his and held it, like it was truly precious. 'First things first. I've come home.'

How was a girl to respond to that? She couldn't.

'I was born here,' he said, taking no obvious offence at her silence, but ploughing on regardless. 'I suspect I was con-ceived in the house over there. As you were conceived here. They say there's a strong chance you end up marrying the girl next door. How about that?'

Whoa! She should say something, she thought. But what? What?

'But I'm getting ahead of myself,' he said, smiling. It was a teasing smile. It was the smile she loved with all her heart.

'I've quit my job,' he told her. 'For the past two months I've been undertaking intensive post-graduate training in pain management. There's more to learn, but instead of being an anaesthetist who's good at managing pain, what I've decided to do is to become a pain management specialist. I need more training still, but I can learn it on the job, and I can learn it here. I can be useful now. I can be useful here.'

And then, as surprise did give her something to say, he pressured her hand, telling her there was more to come, that for now he simply needed her to listen.

'Tori, I was brought up believing my father didn't care,' he told her. 'My mother didn't care either—not emotionally—and that left me with nothing. Or maybe I had emotions, but I learned to lock them away. And then I found you, breaking your heart over a dead koala. And I found the community of Combadeen. I found people who'd loved my father and who he'd loved in turn. I discovered that I'd been raised on a lie.'

He tugged her hand then, just a little so she turned and was facing him.

'None of that matters,' he said, 'except in explaining why I was so long in seeing what was before my eyes. When you left I kept going to work, telling myself I was dumb, only you'd left me colour, all through my apartment.'

'I knew you'd like it,' she interrupted, absurdly pleased.

'I love it,' he said simply. 'I've had it all shipped here. And I love Ferdy and Freddy. They're already in quarantine. I'm hoping Itsy, Bitsy and Rusty take kindly to them. They're very bossy cats.'

She was almost beyond hearing. She was so confused she felt dizzy. He was shipping his life…here?

'You're coming here?'

'I'm here.'

'You can't.'

'Why can't I?'

'Your life's in Manhattan.'

'My life's with you.'

There was a heart stopper if ever she heard one. Her heart definitely stopped, and it took time before she got it going again. And when she did…

Caution, she thought. Don't get your hopes up. This can't be what it seems.

'Jake, we can organise access some other way,' she managed. 'I mean…I know you want a say in how our baby's raised.'

'I want more than that,' he said, strongly and surely. 'I want to see him wake up in the morning and I want to read him bedtime stories. I want to make sure he's taught baseball and not indoctrinated into that very curious game you call football. I want—'

'To change diapers?'

'That, too,' he said, and he didn't even smile. It seemed he was deadly serious. 'I want to share in getting up in the middle of the night. I want to cope with dramas. I want to go to school plays. Did you know my mother never went to a single one of my school plays? Not a one. I'm going to the lot.'

'Does this mean I don't have to?' she asked, trying to joke, but it didn't work. There was too much at stake here for laughter.

'I suspect it's a team effort,' he said softly, seriously. 'The mother and father need to sit together.'

'Jake…'

'I know it's too fast,' he said, quickly now, as if he was afraid she'd stop him before she'd heard him out. 'I know we've barely had more than our five-minute date. But I want to put a proposition before you.'

He rose, and tugged her to her feet, then led her through the cleared area where once her home had stood. To a spot at the northern end.

'This was the kitchen, right?' he said, and she nodded.

'So this view…it'll have been where you stood and looked out as a family, as you cooked, as you washed dishes, as you lived.'

'Yes.'

'Then there's a choice to be made,' he said softly. 'As I said at the beginning, there're three options.'

'Three.'

'Number one,' he said, moving right on. 'That you fall into my arms right this minute, and we go next door and we move into what was my father's home and we live happily ever after. It's only my preferred option because it's the quickest,' he said hurriedly. 'But no pressure. I came up before and opened the windows and made it smell great, and I think it looks great, but if you don't want—'

'Jake…'

'You need to listen to all three before you decide,' he told her, trying to sound severe. 'And you need to listen to the plans in full. If we did that—if lived next door—then I think we should build the world's best wildlife shelter here, plus a clinic for the work you used to do. Caring for the horses that used to live up here and will live up here again. Families are returning, Tori. Life's starting here again.'

'But—'

'And we could call it after the dogs you lost,' he said gently. 'Mutsy and Pogo and Bandit's Animal Care. Big letters out the front. Every care in the world inside.'

'Oh, Jake…'

'Or two,' he said hurriedly, and maybe he thought she was about to burst into tears. She might, she thought mistily. She just might. But for now it was more important to listen.

'Okay, moving right onto option two,' he said, and his grip on her hands became more urgent. 'Option two's if you decide you still want to live here. But even if you did want to live here, you'd agree that I could live here, too. I've thought that one through. If you did that, then we could turn next door, my place, into Mutsy and Pogo and Bandit's Animal Care. It'd take a bit more work, as we have a house there and a blank canvas here, and it'd be a bit of a waste of new curtains, but it could be done. If you want this to stay as your kitchen view, my love, then that's your option.'

'Your love?' It was a squeak. It was definitely a squeak.

'Definitely my love,' he said, and he tugged her tight against him. 'And then there lies option three. Because much as I love you, much as I admit that my five-minute date was the best thing that could ever have happened to me, much as I want you to be beside me for the rest of my life, if you don't want that, or you're not ready, or you think you could do better, then I'll help you rebuild here, and I'll live next door so I can still teach Hildebrand to play baseball...'

'Hildebrand?'

'We have some discussion to do,' he said lovingly. 'Lots of discussion.'

'Jake...'

'Yes?'

She was trying to get her head around this. Her head wasn't big enough to take it in.

'You'd live up here? And work...in Melbourne?'

'In the valley. As Susie says, there's work and to spare. She's already set up discussions with health-care providers. I can start work tomorrow if I want. I'll need to go back and forth to the city for further training but that's feasible. You could come with me. And I need to take a few weeks off before I start. I have a half-grown dog to train.'

'Jake, stop.'

'It's too fast,' he said, suddenly rueful. 'I promised myself I wouldn't pressure you. Those three options—you can take your time, my love. You can have our baby and we can decide then. I won't coerce you into falling into my arms because I want to be a father. Because I want to be your husband first. That's what I want most. Everything else can wait.'

And then, because she didn't speak, because she couldn't, he smiled and suddenly lifted her up into his arms and he carried her across the scraped-up earth that was all that was left of her past life, and he took her to where the fireplace still stood, a blackened sentinel in the centre of what once had been her home.

The chimney stood, charred and blackened, the massive mantel that had straddled it still there, burned and twisted but still recognisably a mantel.

And on the blackened timber, a crimson box.

'This is for later,' Jake said softly, and he set her down. 'I came up here on the way to find you, and I left this here and I made a vow. I'd help you rebuild your life, my love, and if at any stage of the rebuilding you think, Maybe I wouldn't mind a man in my life, then this little box will be here. It'll sit here waiting so that I won't have to wait for the right time. Any sliver of opportunity and I'm in.'

'You...you just left it here?'

'There were three wallabies here when I got here,' Jake said. 'They promised they'd guard it. You want a look?

And what was a girl to say to that?

'It's not as big as the one at Tiffany's,' he said, suddenly anxious. 'And it's presumptuous.'

'I only want a peek.' She could almost laugh at the look on his face. Almost but not quite.

So he flipped it open.

It was like the one at Tiffany's.

He'd had it copied exactly. A glistening solitaire diamond in the centre, a heart, then five tiny rubies, with the thinnest ring of diamonds forming the outer edge of the heart. It had all the beauty of the one she'd seen but none of the ostentation. It was exquisite.

Her heart seemed to still, settle, warm....

But then, as she put her finger down to touch, he tugged it back and the lid snapped closed with a firm little click. Back it went, onto its resting place of charred timber, a crimson slash against the black.

'It's too soon,' he said, sounding firm. 'Far too soon. It's to sit there, Tori, until it's not too soon. It's to stay there until you know your heart, and if it stays there until we're old and grey, it's okay, I'll still be waiting.'

She started up at him, speechless, and she knew he was absolutely serious.

No pressure. She could live here again for as long as she wanted, and he'd be next door, the father to her child, doctor to this community.

The man she loved.

Was it too soon?

And she knew.

Five-minute dating? She didn't need five minutes, she thought mistily, and she put both her hands on Jake's shoulders and she pushed him sideways, so hard he staggered. She grinned, for her way was clear now. There were no barriers between herself and the blackened hearth.

'If you don't mind,' she said softly, wondrously, even finding room for laughter. 'You're getting in the way of my heart's desire.'

And she stepped forwards and retrieved the box, and she slid the ring on her finger before Jake could produce any more dumb arguments about too soon and wait and which path would she go.

For she knew her own path. With Jake's ring on her finger she turned to her man, and she stepped into the arms of her heart's desire.

A gleaming new family wagon, bright red, big enough to hold dogs, cats and kids, turned into the gate of the homestead up on the ridge—Old Doc's Place, according to the locals—and drew to a halt.

Jake climbed out, went round to the passenger side to help his wife out of the car and then together they lifted the baby capsule from the back seat.

Charlotte Elizabeth Hunter gazed up at her parents, wide-eyed and wondering. They smiled down at her, they smiled at each other and together they carried their brand-new baby into her home.

The dogs were waiting to meet them. Itsy and Bitsy and the boss of the pack, Rusty, were quivering with excitement, but the pecking order had been established months ago. Ferdy and Freddy came first, prancing down the steps in stately dignity to investigate this new little member of their family. When the cats conceded their places—after cautious approval—the dogs wriggled and bounced and shivered their pleasure until Jake ordered control.

'Back,' Jake said and the dogs backed, just like that. They were beautifully trained. They'd been trained by Jake, under instruction from Tori. A team effort.

This whole place was a team effort, Jake thought in satisfaction. There were delicious smells coming from the kitchen. Doreen and Glenda had been here this morning, to make sure everything was perfect, then slipping away before they arrived, to give them some privacy.

There was team effort everywhere. Through the regenerating bushland, Jake could just see signs of activity next door. The new Mutsy and Pogo and Bandit's Animal Care Centre was up and running, in the place where Tori's house had once stood.

'I don't mind moving,' she'd said, choosing Option One with alacrity. 'Home is where the heart is, after all.'

Home.

He knew what it was now, he thought, as he ushered his new wife inside, as he carried his new child into her new home.

Home.

It didn't go with the concept of alone.

Home was dogs, he thought, and cats, and a goldfish called Jake. Home was friends, neighbours, community.

Home was colour and comfort and a fire, and toast on Sunday morning, and great coffee, or no coffee at all because someone had forgotten to buy it. So home might also be hot chocolate, and cleaning up after the dogs and yelling at the cockatoos who were intent on stripping the paintwork off the verandah.

Home was patients dropping in, and friends.

Home was life.

'So now we get to live happily every after?' he said to Tori, settling Charlotte Elizabeth on the settee and wondering vaguely what they were going to do with her. Parents coped with newborns all the time, he thought. It couldn't be that hard.

Then there was a knock on the door, and frenzied barking. He and Tori looked at each other and sighed, and Jake opened the door.

A little girl was there, twelve maybe, and behind her was a horse, about three times the size of her. The horse was being held by a guy who looked like a farmer.

'Please…' the little girl whispered and looked past Jake to Tori.

'Yes?' Tori said. She'd scooped Charlotte up and was cradling her. She looked beautiful, Jake thought. His Tori.

'My horse stood on a nail,' the little girl said. 'It's really deep. Dad said…Dad said he knew you had a little baby and cats, and the odd wombat with an injured paw—but if we brought Prince to you, maybe you could just see…'

'I'm real sorry,' the man called out. 'It's just…having New Doc's Place so close now… It'd save us trailering her down to the city, and it'd be simple, I think. If it's okay. And the wife's sent a sponge cake.'

And to Jake's astonishment—or maybe not, because he should be used to it by now—Tori was smiling. Smiling and smiling.

'It's fine,' she said, and before Jake knew what she intended, Charlotte was in his arms. 'My husband can take care of our baby,' she told the farmer. 'I'll just get my bag.'

So Jake was left, holding his baby—who was starting to feel wet—and a plate of chocolate sponge cake. He stood on the verandah of their new home, while Tori did her vet thing, while the community went on around them, while his dogs slept at his feet.

And he smiled, too.

Home is where the heart is.

Home is here.

™MILLS & BOON®

SEPTEMBER 2010 HARDBACK TITLES

ROMANCE

HISTORICAL

MEDICAL™

0810 Gen Std LP

MILLS & BOON

SEPTEMBER 2010 LARGE PRINT TITLES

ROMANCE

Virgin on Her Wedding Night	Lynne Graham
Blackwolf's Redemption	Sandra Marton
The Shy Bride	Lucy Monroe
Penniless and Purchased	Julia James
Beauty and the Reclusive Prince	Raye Morgan
Executive: Expecting Tiny Twins	Barbara Hannay
A Wedding at Leopard Tree Lodge	Liz Fielding
Three Times A Bridesmaid...	Nicola Marsh

HISTORICAL

The Viscount's Unconventional Bride	Mary Nichols
Compromising Miss Milton	Michelle Styles
Forbidden Lady	Anne Herries

MEDICAL™

The Doctor's Lost-and-Found Bride	Kate Hardy
Miracle: Marriage Reunited	Anne Fraser
A Mother for Matilda	Amy Andrews
The Boss and Nurse Albright	Lynne Marshall
New Surgeon at Ashvale A&E	Joanna Neil
Desert King, Doctor Daddy	Meredith Webber

0910 Gen Std HB

MILLS & BOON

OCTOBER 2010 HARDBACK TITLES

ROMANCE

The Reluctant Surrender	Penny Jordan
Shameful Secret, Shotgun Wedding	Sharon Kendrick
The Virgin's Choice	Jennie Lucas
Scandal: Unclaimed Love-Child	Melanie Milburne
Powerful Greek, Housekeeper Wife	Robyn Donald
Hired by Her Husband	Anne McAllister
Snowbound Seduction	Helen Brooks
A Mistake, A Prince and A Pregnancy	Maisey Yates
Champagne with a Celebrity	Kate Hardy
When He was Bad...	Anne Oliver
Accidentally Pregnant!	Rebecca Winters
Star-Crossed Sweethearts	Jackie Braun
A Miracle for His Secret Son	Barbara Hannay
Proud Rancher, Precious Bundle	Donna Alward
Cowgirl Makes Three	Myrna Mackenzie
Secret Prince, Instant Daddy!	Raye Morgan
Officer, Surgeon...Gentleman!	Janice Lynn
Midwife in the Family Way	Fiona McArthur

HISTORICAL

Innocent Courtesan to Adventurer's Bride	Louise Allen
Disgrace and Desire	Sarah Mallory
The Viking's Captive Princess	Michelle Styles

MEDICAL™

Bachelor of the Baby Ward	Meredith Webber
Fairytale on the Children's Ward	Meredith Webber
Playboy Under the Mistletoe	Joanna Neil
Their Marriage Miracle	Sue MacKay

0910 Gen Std LP

MILLS & BOON®

OCTOBER 2010 LARGE PRINT TITLES

ROMANCE

Marriage: To Claim His Twins	Penny Jordan
The Royal Baby Revelation	Sharon Kendrick
Under the Spaniard's Lock and Key	Kim Lawrence
Sweet Surrender with the Millionaire	Helen Brooks
Miracle for the Girl Next Door	Rebecca Winters
Mother of the Bride	Caroline Anderson
What's A Housekeeper To Do?	Jennie Adams
Tipping the Waitress with Diamonds	Nina Harrington

HISTORICAL

Practical Widow to Passionate Mistress	Louise Allen
Major Westhaven's Unwilling Ward	Emily Bascom
Her Banished Lord	Carol Townend

MEDICAL™

The Nurse's Brooding Boss	Laura Iding
Emergency Doctor and Cinderella	Melanie Milburne
City Surgeon, Small Town Miracle	Marion Lennox
Bachelor Dad, Girl Next Door	Sharon Archer
A Baby for the Flying Doctor	Lucy Clark
Nurse, Nanny...Bride!	Alison Roberts